1 3 5 7 9 10 8 6 4 2

Vintage
20 Vauxhall Bridge Road,
London SW1V 2SA

Vintage Classics is part of the Penguin Random House
group of companies whose addresses can be found at
global.penguinrandomhouse.com.

Penguin
Random House
UK

Song of Solomon first published in Great Britain by Chatto & Windus in 1978
The Bluest Eye first published in Great Britain by Chatto & Windus in 1979
Beloved first published in Great Britain by Chatto & Windus in 1987
'Recitatif' first published in *Confirmation: An Anthology of
African American Women* in 1983
'Make America White Again' originally published in the *New Yorker*, 2016
This short edition published by Vintage in 2017

penguin.co.uk/vintage

A CIP catalogue record for this book is available from the British Library

ISBN 9781784872779

Typeset in 9.5/14.5 pt FreightText Pro
by Jouve (UK), Milton Keynes
Printed and bound by Clays Ltd, St Ives plc

Penguin Random House is committed to a sustainable future for
our business, our readers and our planet. This book is made from
Forest Stewardship Council® certified paper.

Race

TONI MORRISON

VINTAGE MINIS

From the novel *Song of Solomon*

AT FIFTY-TWO, MACON Dead was as imposing a man as
he had been at forty-two, when Milkman thought he was
the biggest thing in the world. Bigger even than the house
they lived in. But today he had seen a woman who was just
as tall and who had made him feel tall too.

'I know I'm the youngest one in this family, but I ain't
no baby. You treat me like I was a baby. You keep saying
you don't have to explain nothing to me. How do you
think that makes me feel? Like a baby, that's what. Like a
twelve-year-old baby!'

'Don't you raise your voice to me.'

'Is that the way your father treated you when you
were twelve?'

'Watch your mouth!' Macon roared. He took his hands
out of his pockets but didn't know what to do with them.
He was momentarily confused. His son's question had
shifted the scenery. He was seeing himself at twelve,
standing in Milkman's shoes and feeling what he himself

had felt for his own father. The numbness that had settled on him when he saw the man he loved and admired fall off the fence; something wild ran through him when he watched the body twitching in the dirt. His father had sat for five nights on a split-rail fence cradling a shotgun and in the end died protecting his property. Was that what this boy felt for him? Maybe it was time to tell him things.

'Well, did he?'

'I worked right alongside my father. Right alongside him. From the time I was four or five we worked together. Just the two of us. Our mother was dead. Died when Pilate was born. Pilate was just a baby. She stayed over at another farm in the daytime. I carried her over there myself in my arms every morning. Then I'd go back across the fields and meet my father. We'd hitch President Lincoln to the plow and . . . That's what we called her: President Lincoln. Papa said Lincoln was a good plow hand before he was President and you shouldn't take a good plow hand away from his work. He called our farm Lincoln's Heaven. It was a little bit a place. But it looked big to me then. I know now it must a been a little bit a place, maybe a hundred and fifty acres. We tilled fifty. About eighty of it was woods. Must of been a fortune in oak and pine; maybe that's what they wanted – the lumber, the oak and the pine. We had a pond that was four acres. And a stream, full of fish. Right down in the heart of a valley. Prettiest mountain you ever saw, Montour Ridge. We lived in Montour County. Just north of the Susquehanna. We had a four-stall hog pen. The big barn was forty feet by a hundred and forty – hip-roofed too. And all around in the mountains was deer and wild turkey. You ain't tasted nothing till you taste wild turkey the way Papa cooked it. He'd burn it real fast in the fire. Burn it black all over. That sealed it. Sealed the juices in. Then he'd let it roast on a spit for twenty-four hours. When you cut the black burnt part off, the meat underneath was tender, sweet, juicy. And we had fruit trees. Apple, cherry. Pilate tried to make me a cherry pie once.'

Macon paused and let the smile come on. He had not said any of this for years. Had not even reminisced much about it recently. When he was first married he used to talk about Lincoln's Heaven to Ruth. Sitting on the porch swing in the dark, he would re-create the land that was to have been his. Or when he was just starting out in the business of buying houses, he would lounge around the barbershop and swap stories with the men there. But for years he hadn't had that kind of time, or interest. But now he was doing it again, with his son, and every detail of that land was clear in his mind: the well, the apple orchard, President Lincoln; her foal, Mary Todd; Ulysses S. Grant, their cow; General Lee, their hog. That was the way he knew what history he remembered. His father couldn't read, couldn't write; knew only what he saw and heard tell of. But he had etched in Macon's mind certain historical figures, and as a boy in school, Macon thought of the personalities of his horse, his hog, when he read about these people. His father may have called their plow horse President Lincoln as a joke, but Macon always thought of Lincoln with fondness since he had loved him first as a strong, steady, gentle, and obedient horse. He even liked General Lee, for one spring they slaughtered him and ate the best pork outside Virginia, 'from the butt to the smoked ham to the ribs to the sausage to the jowl to the feet to the tail to the head cheese' – for eight months. And there was cracklin in November.

'General Lee was all right by me,' he told Milkman, smiling. 'Finest general I ever knew. Even his balls was tasty. Circe made up the best pot of maws she ever cooked. Huh! I'd forgotten that woman's name. That was it, Circe. Worked at a big farm some white people owned in Danville, Pennsylvania. Funny how things get away from you. For years you can't remember nothing. Then just like that, it all comes back to you. Had a dog run, they did. That was the big sport back then. Dog races. White people did love their dogs. Kill a nigger and comb their hair at the same time. But I've seen grown white men cry about their dogs.'

His voice sounded different to Milkman. Less hard, and his speech was different. More southern and comfortable and soft. Milkman spoke softly too. 'Pilate said somebody shot your father. Five feet into the air.'

'Took him sixteen years to get that farm to where it was paying. It's all dairy country up there now. Then it wasn't. Then it was . . . nice.'

'Who shot him, Daddy?'

Macon focused his eyes on his son. 'Papa couldn't read, couldn't even sign his name. Had a mark he used. They tricked him. He signed something, I don't know what, and they told him they owned his property. He never read nothing. I tried to teach him, but he said he couldn't remember those little marks from one day to the next. Wrote one word in his life – Pilate's name; copied it out of the Bible. That's what she got folded up in that earring. He should have let me teach him. Everything bad that ever happened to him happened because he couldn't read. Got his name messed up cause he couldn't read.'

'His name? How?'

'When freedom came. All the colored people in the state had to register with the Freedmen's Bureau.'

'Your father was a slave?'

'What kind of foolish question is that? Course he was. Who hadn't been in 1869? They all had to register. Free and not free. Free and used-to-be-slaves. Papa was in his teens and went to sign up, but the man behind the desk was drunk. He asked Papa where he was born. Papa said Macon. Then he asked him who his father was. Papa said, "He's dead." Asked him who owned him, Papa said, "I'm free." Well, the Yankee wrote it all down, but in the wrong spaces. Had him born in Dunfrie, wherever the hell that is, and in the space for his name the fool wrote, "Dead" comma "Macon." But Papa couldn't read so he never found out what he was registered as till Mama told him.

They met on a wagon going North. Started talking about one thing and another, told her about being a freedman and showed off his papers to her. When she looked at his paper she read him out what it said.'

'He didn't have to keep the name, did he? He could have used his real name, couldn't he?'

'Mama liked it. Liked the name. Said it was new and would wipe out the past. Wipe it all out.'

'What was his real name?'

'I don't remember my mother too well. She died when I was four. Light-skinned, pretty. Looked like a white woman to me. Me and Pilate don't take nothing after her. If you ever have a doubt we from Africa, look at Pilate. She look just like Papa and he looked like all them pictures you ever see of Africans. A Pennsylvania African. Acted like one too. Close his face up like a door.'

'I saw Pilate's face like that.' Milkman felt close and confidential now that his father had talked to him in a relaxed and intimate way.

'I haven't changed my mind, Macon. I don't want you over there.'

'Why? You still haven't said why.'

'Just listen to what I say. That woman's no good. She's a snake, and can charm you like a snake, but still a snake.'

'You talking about your own sister, the one you carried in your arms to the fields every morning.'

'That was a long time ago. You seen her. What she look like to you? Somebody nice? Somebody normal?'

'Well, she . . .'

'Or somebody cut your throat?'

'She didn't look like that, Daddy.'

'Well she *is* like that.'

'What'd she do?'

'It ain't what she did; it's what she is.'

'What is she?'

'A snake, I told you. Ever hear the story about the snake? The man who saw a little baby snake on the ground? Well, the man saw this baby snake bleeding and hurt. Lying there in the dirt. And the man felt sorry for it and picked it up and put it in his basket and took it home. And he fed it and took care of it till it was big and strong. Fed it the same thing he ate. Then one day, the snake turned on him and bit him. Stuck his poison tongue right in the man's heart. And while he was laying there dying, he turned to the snake and asked him, "What'd you do that for?" He said, "Didn't I take good care of you? Didn't I save your life?" The snake said, "Yes." "Then what'd you do it for? What'd you kill me for?" Know what the snake said? Said, "But you knew I was a snake, didn't you?" Now, I mean for you to stay out of that wine house and as far away from Pilate as you can.'

Milkman lowered his head. His father had explained nothing to him.

'Boy, you got better things to do with your time. Besides, it's time you started learning how to work. You start Monday. After school come to my office; work a couple of hours there and learn what's real. Pilate can't teach you a thing you can use in this world. Maybe the next, but not this one. Let me tell you right now the one important thing you'll ever need to know: Own things. And let the things you own own other things. Then you'll own yourself and other people too. Starting Monday, I'm going to teach you how.'

THEY WERE SITTING in Mary's Place on a Sunday afternoon a few days after Hagar's latest attempt on his life.

'You're not smoking?' asked Milkman.

'No. I quit. Feel a hell of a lot better too.' There was another pause before Guitar continued. 'You ought to stop yourself.'

Milkman nodded. 'Yeah. If I stay around you I will. I'll stop smoking, fucking, drinking – everything. I'll take up a secret life and hanging out with Empire State.'

Guitar frowned. 'Now who's meddling?'

Milkman sighed and looked straight at his friend. 'I am. I want to know why you were running around with Empire State last Christmas.'

'He was in trouble. I helped him.'

'That's all?'

'What else?'

'I don't know what else. But I know there is something else. Now, if it's something I can't know, okay, say so. But something's going on with you. And I'd like to know what it is.'

Guitar didn't answer.

'We've been friends a long time, Guitar. There's nothing you don't know about me. I can tell you anything – whatever our differences, I know I can trust you. But for some time now it's been a one-way street. You know what I mean? I talk to you, but you don't talk to me. You don't think I can be trusted?'

'I don't know if you can or not.'

'Try me.'

'I can't. Other people are involved.'

'Then don't tell me about other people; tell me about you.'

Guitar looked at him for a long time. Maybe, he thought. Maybe I can trust you. Maybe not, but I'll risk it anyway because one day . . .

'Okay,' he said aloud, 'but you have to know that what I tell you can't go any further. And if it does, you'll be dropping a rope around my neck. Now do you still want to know it?'

'Yeah.'

'You sure?'

'I'm sure.'

Guitar poured some more hot water over his tea. He looked into his cup for a minute while the leaves settled slowly to the bottom. 'I suppose you know that white people kill black people from time to time, and most folks shake their heads and say, "Eh, eh, eh, ain't that a shame?"'

Milkman raised his eyebrows. He thought Guitar was

going to let him in on some deal he had going. But he was slipping into his race bag. He was speaking slowly, as though each word had to count, and as though he were listening carefully to his own words. 'I can't suck my teeth or say "Eh, eh, eh." I had to do something. And the only thing left to do is balance it; keep things on an even keel. Any man, any woman, or any child is good for five to seven generations of heirs before they're bred out. So every death is the death of five to seven generations. You can't stop them from killing us, from trying to get rid of us. And each time they succeed, they get rid of five to seven generations. I help keep the numbers the same.

'There is a society. It's made up of a few men who are willing to take some risks. They don't initiate anything; they don't even choose. They are as indifferent as rain. But when a Negro child, Negro woman, or Negro man is killed by whites and nothing is done about it by *their* law and *their* courts, this society selects a similar victim at random, and they execute him or her in a similar manner if they can. If the Negro was hanged, they hang; if a Negro was burnt, they burn; raped and murdered, they rape and murder. If they can. If they can't do it precisely in the same manner, they do it any way they can, but they do it. They call themselves the Seven Days. They are made up of seven men. Always seven and only seven. If one of them dies or leaves or is no longer effective, another is chosen. Not right away, because that kind of choosing takes time. But they don't seem to be in a hurry. Their secret is time. To take the time, to last. Not to grow; that's dangerous because you might become known. They don't write their names in toilet stalls or brag to women. Time and silence. Those are their weapons, and they go on forever.

'It got started in 1920, when that private from Georgia was killed after his balls were cut off and after that veteran was blinded when he came home from France in World War I. And it's been operating ever since. I am one of them now.'

Milkman had held himself very still all the time Guitar spoke. Now he felt tight, shriveled, and cold.

'You? You're going to kill people?'

'Not people. White people.'

'But why?'

'I just told you. It's necessary; it's got to be done. To keep the ratio the same.'

'And if it isn't done? If it just goes on the way it has?'

'Then the world is a zoo, and I can't live in it.'

'Why don't you just hunt down the ones who did the killing? Why kill innocent people? Why not just those who did it?'

'It doesn't matter who did it. Each and every one of them could do it. So you just get any one of them. There are no innocent white people, because every one of them is a potential nigger-killer, if not an actual one. You think Hitler surprised them? You think just because they went to war they thought he was a freak? Hitler's the most natural white man in the world. He killed Jews and Gypsies because he didn't have us. Can you see those Klansmen shocked by him? No, you can't.'

'But people who lynch and slice off people's balls – they're crazy, Guitar, crazy.'

'Every time somebody does a thing like that to one of us, they say the people who did it were crazy or ignorant. That's like saying they were drunk. Or constipated. Why isn't cutting a man's eyes out, cutting his nuts off, the kind of thing you never get too drunk or ignorant to do? Too crazy to do? Too constipated to do? And more to the point, how come Negroes, the craziest, most ignorant people in America, don't get that crazy and that ignorant? No. White people are unnatural. As a race they are unnatural. And it takes a strong effort of the will to overcome an unnatural enemy.'

'What about the nice ones? Some whites made sacrifices for Negroes. Real sacrifices.'

'That just means there are one or two natural ones. But they haven't been able to stop the killing either. They are outraged, but that doesn't stop it. They might even speak out, but that doesn't stop it either. They might even inconvenience themselves, but the killing goes on and on. So will we.'

'You're missing the point. There're not just one or two. There're a lot.'

'Are there? Milkman, if Kennedy got drunk and bored and was sitting around a potbellied stove in Mississippi, he might join a lynching party just for the hell of it. Under those circumstances his unnaturalness would surface. But I know I wouldn't join one no matter how drunk I was or how bored, and I know you wouldn't either, nor any black man I know or ever heard tell of. Ever. In any world, at any time, just get up and go find somebody white to slice up. But they *can* do it. And they don't even do it for profit, which is why they do most things. They do it for fun. Unnatural.'

'What about . . .' Milkman searched his memory for some white person who had shown himself unequivocally supportive of Negroes. 'Schweitzer. Albert Schweitzer. Would he do it?'

'In a minute. He didn't care anything about those Africans. They could have been rats. He was in a laboratory testing *himself* – proving he could work on human dogs.'

'What about Eleanor Roosevelt?'

'I don't know about the women. I can't say what their women would do, but I do remember that picture of those white mothers holding up their babies so they could get a good look at some black men burning on a tree. So I have my suspicions about Eleanor Roosevelt. But *none* about Mr Roosevelt. You could've taken him and his wheelchair and put him in a small dusty town in Alabama and given him some tobacco, a checkerboard, some whiskey, and a rope and he'd have done it too. What I'm saying is, under certain conditions they would *all* do it. And under the same circumstances we would not. So it doesn't matter that some of them *haven't* done it. I listen. I read. And now

I know that they know it too. They know they are unnatural. Their writers and artists have been saying it for years. Telling them they are unnatural, telling them they are depraved. They call it tragedy. In the movies they call it adventure. It's just depravity that they try to make glorious, natural. But it ain't. The disease they have is in their blood, in the structure of their chromosomes.'

'You can prove this, I guess. Scientifically?'

'No.'

'Shouldn't you be able to prove it before you act on something like that?'

'Did they prove anything scientifically about us before they killed us? No. They killed us first and then tried to get some scientific proof about why we should die.'

'Wait a minute, Guitar. If they are as bad, as unnatural, as you say, why do you want to be like them? Don't you want to be better than they are?'

'I am better.'

'But now you're doing what the worst of them do.'

'Yes, but I am reasonable.'

'Reasonable? How?'

'I am not, one, having fun; two, trying to gain power or public attention or money or land; three, angry at anybody.'

'You're not angry? You must be!'

'Not at all. I hate doing it. I'm afraid to do it. It's hard to do it when you aren't angry or drunk or doped up or don't have a personal grudge against the person.'

'I can't see how it helps. I can't see how it helps anybody.'

'I told you. Numbers. Balance. Ratio. And the earth, the land.'

'I'm not understanding you.'

'The earth is soggy with black people's blood. And before us Indian blood. Nothing can cure them, and if it keeps on there won't be any of us left and there won't be any land for those who are left. So the numbers have to remain static.'

'But there are more of them than us.'

'Only in the West. But still the ratio can't widen in their favor.'

'But you should want everybody to know that the society exists. Then maybe that would help stop it. What's the secrecy for?'

'To keep from getting caught.'

'Can't you even let other Negroes know about it? I mean to give us hope?'

'No.'

'Why not?'

'Betrayal. The possibility of betrayal.'

'Well, let *them* know. Let white people know. Like the Mafia or the Klan; frighten them into behaving.'

'You're talking foolishness. How can you let one group know and not the other? Besides, we are not like them. The Mafia is unnatural. So is the Klan. One kills for money, the other kills for fun. And they have huge profits and protection at their disposal. We don't. But it's not about other people knowing. We don't even tell the victims. We just whisper to him, "Your Day has come." The beauty of what we do is its secrecy, its smallness. The fact that nobody needs the unnatural satisfaction of talking about it. Telling about it. We don't discuss it among ourselves, the details. We just get an assignment. If the Negro was killed on a Wednesday, the Wednesday man takes it; if he was killed on Monday, the Monday man takes that one. And we just notify one another when it's completed, not how or who. And if it ever gets to be too much, like it was for Robert Smith, we do *that* rather than crack and tell somebody. Like Porter. It was getting him down. They thought somebody would have to take over his day. He just needed a rest and he's okay now.'

Milkman stared at his friend and then let the spasm he had been holding back run through him. 'I can't buy it, Guitar.'

'I know that.'

'There's too much wrong with it.'

'Tell me.'

'Well, for one thing, you'll get caught eventually.'

'Maybe. But if I'm caught I'll just die earlier than I'm supposed to – not better than I'm supposed to. And how I die or when doesn't interest me. What I die *for* does. It's the same as what I live for. Besides, if I'm caught they'll accuse me and kill me for one crime, maybe two, never for all. And there are still six other days in the week. We've been around for a long long time. And believe me, we'll be around for a long long time to come.'

'You can't marry.'

'No.'

'Have children.'

'No.'

'What kind of life is that?'

'Very satisfying.'

'There's no love in it.'

'No love? No love? Didn't you hear me? What I'm doing ain't about hating white people. It's about loving us. About loving you. My whole life is love.'

'Man, you're confused.'

'Am I? When those concentration camp Jews hunt down Nazis, are they hating Nazis or loving dead Jews?'

'It's not the same thing.'

'Only because they have money and publicity.'

'No; because they turn them over to the courts. You kill and you don't kill the killers. You kill innocent people.'

'I told you there are no –'

'And you don't correct a thing by –'

'We poor people, Milkman. I work at an auto plant. The rest of us barely eke out a living. Where's the money, the state, the country to finance our justice? You say Jews try their catches in a court. Do we have a court? Is there one courthouse in one city in the country where a jury would convict them? There are places right now where a Negro still can't testify against a white man. Where the judge, the jury, the court, are legally bound to ignore anything a Negro has to say. What that means is that a black man is a victim of a crime only when a white man says he is. Only then. If there was anything like or near justice or courts when a cracker kills a Negro, there wouldn't have to be no Seven Days. But there ain't; so we are. And we do it without money, without support, without costumes, without newspapers, without senators, without lobbyists, and without illusions!'

'You sound like that red-headed Negro named X. Why don't you join him and call yourself Guitar X?'

'X, Bains – what difference does it make? I don't give a damn about names.'

'You miss his point. His point is to let white people know you don't accept your slave name.'

'I don't give a shit what white people know or even think. Besides, I do accept it. It's part of who I am. Guitar is *my* name. Bains is the slave master's name. And I'm all of that. Slave names don't bother me; but slave status does.'

'And knocking off white folks changes your slave status?'

'Believe it.'

'Does it do anything for my slave status?'

Guitar smiled. 'Well, doesn't it?'

'Hell, no.' Milkman frowned. 'Am I going to live any longer because you all read the newspaper and then ambush some poor old white man?'

'It's not about you living longer. It's about how you live and why. It's about whether your children can make other children. It's about trying to make a world where one day white people will think before they lynch.'

'Guitar, none of that shit is going to change how I live or how any other Negro lives. What you're doing is crazy. And something else: it's a habit. If you do it enough, you can do it to anybody. You know what I mean? A torpedo is a torpedo, I don't care what his reasons. You can off anybody you don't like. You can off me.'

'We don't off Negroes.'

'You hear what you said? *Negroes*. Not Milkman. Not "No, I can't touch *you*, Milkman," but "We don't off Negroes." Shit, man, suppose you all change your parliamentary rules?'

'The Days are the Days. It's been that way a long time.'

Milkman thought about that. 'Any other young dudes in it? Are all the others older? You the only young one?'

'Why?'

''Cause young dudes are subject to change the rules.'

'You worried about yourself, Milkman?' Guitar looked amused.

'No. Not really.' Milkman put his cigarette out and reached for another one. 'Tell me, what's your day?'

'Sunday. I'm the Sunday man.'

Milkman rubbed the ankle of his short leg. 'I'm scared for you, man.'

'That's funny. I'm scared for you too.'

GUITAR WAS WATCHING him carefully. 'What's the matter?' he asked. 'Why you so low? You don't act like a man on his way to the end of the rainbow.'

Milkman turned around and sat on the sill. 'I hope it *is* a rainbow, and nobody has run off with the pot, cause I need it.'

'Everybody needs it.'

'Not as bad as me.'

Guitar smiled. 'Look like you really got the itch now. More than before.'

'Yeah, well, everything's worse than before, or maybe it's the same as before. I don't know. I just know that I want to live my own life. I don't want to be my old man's office boy no more. And as long as I'm in this place I will be. Unless I have my own money. I have to get out of that house and I don't want to owe anybody when I go. My family's driving me crazy. Daddy wants me to be like him and hate my mother. My mother wants me to think like her and hate my father. Corinthians won't speak to me; Lena wants me out. And Hagar wants me chained to her bed or dead. Everybody wants something from me, you know what I mean? Something they think they can't get anywhere else. Something they think I got. I don't know what it is – I mean what it is they really want.'

Guitar stretched his legs. 'They want your life, man.'

'My life?'

'What else?'

'No. Hagar wants my life. My family . . . they want –'

'I don't mean that way. I don't mean they want your dead life; they want your living life.'

'You're losing me,' said Milkman.

'Look. It's the condition our condition is in. Everybody wants the life of a black man. Everybody. White men want us dead or quiet – which is the same thing as dead. White women, same thing. They want us, you know, "universal," human, no "race consciousness." Tame, except in bed. They like a little racial loincloth in the bed. But outside the bed they want us to be individuals. You tell them, "But they lynched my papa," and they say, "Yeah, but you're better than the lynchers are, so forget it." And black women, they want your whole self. Love, they call it, and understanding. "Why don't you *understand* me?" What they mean is, Don't love anything on earth except me. They say, "Be responsible," but what they mean is, Don't go anywhere where I ain't. You try to climb Mount Everest, they'll tie up your ropes. Tell them you want to go to the bottom of the sea – just for a look – they'll hide your oxygen tank. Or you don't even have to go that far. Buy a horn and say you want to play. Oh, they love the music, but only after you pull eight at the post office. Even if you make it, even if you stubborn and mean and you get to the top of Mount Everest, or you do play and you good, real good – that still ain't enough. You blow your lungs out on the horn and they want what breath you got left to hear about how you love them. They want your full attention. Take a risk and they say you not for real. That you don't love them. They won't even let you risk your own life, man, your *own* life – unless it's over them. You can't even die unless it's about them. What good is a man's life if he can't even choose what to die for?'

'Nobody can choose what to die for.'

'Yes you can, and if you can't, you can damn well try to.'

'You sound bitter. If that's what you feel, why are you playing your numbers game? Keeping the racial ratio the same and all? Every time I ask you what you doing it for, you talk about love. Loving Negroes. Now you say –'

'It *is* about love. What else but love? Can't I love what I criticize?'

'Yeah, but except for skin color, I can't tell the difference between what the white women want from us and what the colored women want. You say they all want our life, our living life. So if a colored woman is raped and killed, why do the Days rape and kill a white woman? Why worry about the colored woman at all?'

Guitar cocked his head and looked sideways at Milkman. His nostrils flared a little. 'Because she's *mine*.'

'Yeah. Sure.' Milkman didn't try to keep disbelief out of his voice. 'So everybody wants to kill us, except black men, right?'

'Right.'

'Then why did my father – who is a very black man – try to kill me before I was even born?'

'Maybe he thought you were a little girl; I don't know. But I don't have to tell you that your father is a very strange Negro. He'll reap the benefits of what we sow, and there's nothing we can do about that. He behaves like a

What good is a man's life if he can't even choose what to die for?

white man, thinks like a white man. As a matter of fact, I'm glad you brought him up. Maybe you can tell me how, after losing everything his own father worked for to some crackers, after *seeing* his father shot down by them, how can he keep his knees bent? Why does he love them so? And Pilate. She's worse. She saw it too and, first, goes back to get a cracker's bones for some kind of crazy self-punishment, and second, leaves the cracker's gold right where it was! Now, is that voluntary slavery or not? She slipped into those Jemima shoes cause they fit.'

'Look, Guitar. First of all, my father doesn't care whether a white man lives or swallows lye. He just wants what they have. And Pilate is a little nuts, but she wanted us out of there. If she hadn't been smart, both our asses would be cooling in the joint right now.'

'My ass. Not yours. She wanted you out, not me.'

'Come on. That ain't even fair.'

'No. Fair is one more thing I've given up.'

'But to Pilate? What for? She knew what we did and still she bailed us out. Went down for us, clowned and crawled for us. You saw her face. You ever see anything like it in your life?'

'Once. Just once,' said Guitar. And he remembered anew how his mother smiled when the white man handed her the four ten-dollar bills. More than gratitude was showing in her eyes. More than that. Not love, but a willingness to love. Her husband was sliced in half and boxed backward. He'd heard the mill men tell how the two halves, not even fitted together, were placed cut side down, skin side up, in the coffin. Facing each other. Each eye looking deep into its mate. Each nostril inhaling the breath the other nostril had expelled. The right cheek facing the left. The right elbow crossed over the left elbow. And he had worried then, as a child, that when his father was wakened on Judgment Day his first sight would not be glory or the magnificent head of God – or even the rainbow. It would be his own other eye.

Even so, his mother had smiled and shown that willingness to love the man who was responsible for dividing his father up throughout eternity. It wasn't the divinity from the foreman's wife that made him sick. That came later. It was the fact that instead of life insurance, the sawmill owner gave his mother forty dollars 'to tide you and them kids over,' and she took it happily and bought each of them a big peppermint stick on the very day of the funeral. Guitar's two sisters and baby brother sucked away at the bone-white and blood-red stick, but Guitar couldn't. He held it in his hand until it stuck there. All day he held it. At the graveside, at the funeral supper, all the sleepless night. The others made fun of what they believed was his miserliness, but he could not eat it or throw it away, until finally, in the outhouse, he let it fall into the earth's stinking hole.

'Once,' he said. 'Just once.' And felt the nausea all over again. 'The crunch is here,' he said. 'The big crunch. Don't let them Kennedys fool you. And I'll tell you the truth: I hope your daddy's right about what's in that cave. And I sure hope you don't have no second thoughts about getting it back here.'

'What's that supposed to mean?'

'It means I'm nervous. Real nervous. I need the bread.'

'If you're in a hurt, I can let you have –'

'Not *me*. *Us*. We have work to do, man. And just recently' – Guitar squinted his eyes at Milkman – 'just recently one of us was put out in the streets, by somebody I don't have to name. And his wages were garnisheed cause this somebody said two months rent was owing. This somebody needs two months rent on a twelve-by-twelve hole in the wall like a fish needs side pockets. Now we have to take care of this man, get him a place to stay, pay the so-called back rent, and –'

'That was my fault. Let me tell you what happened . . .'

'No. Don't tell me nothing. You ain't the landlord and you didn't put him out. You may have handed him the gun, but you didn't pull the trigger. I'm not blaming you.'

'Why not? You talk about my father, my father's sister, and you'll talk about my sister too if I let you. Why you trust me?'

'Baby, I hope I never have to ask myself that question.'

It ended all right, that gloomy conversation. There was no real anger and nothing irrevocable was said. When Milkman left, Guitar opened his palm as usual and

Milkman slapped it. Maybe it was fatigue, but the touching of palms seemed a little weak.

MILKMAN TURNED IN his seat and tried to stretch his legs. It was morning. He'd changed buses three times and was now speeding home on the last leg of his trip. He looked out the window. Far away from Virginia, fall had already come. Ohio, Indiana, Michigan were dressed up like the Indian warriors from whom their names came. Blood red and yellow, ocher and ice blue.

He read the road signs with interest now, wondering what lay beneath the names. The Algonquins had named the territory he lived in Great Water, *michi gami*. How many dead lives and fading memories were buried in and beneath the names of the places in this country. Under the recorded names were other names, just as 'Macon Dead,' recorded for all time in some dusty file, hid from view the real names of people, places, and things. Names that had meaning. No wonder Pilate put hers in her ear. When you know your name, you should hang on to it, for unless it is noted down and remembered, it will die when you do. Like the street he lived on, recorded as Mains Avenue, but called Not Doctor Street by the Negroes in memory of his grandfather, who was the first colored man of consequence in that city. Never mind that he probably didn't deserve their honor – they knew what kind of man he was: arrogant, color-struck, snobbish. They didn't care about that. They were paying their respect to whatever it was that made him *be* a doctor in the first place, when the odds were that he'd be a yardman all of his life. So they named a street after him. Pilate had taken a rock from every state she had lived in – because she *had* lived there. And having lived there, it was hers – and his, and his father's, his grandfather's, his grandmother's. Not Doctor Street, Solomon's Leap, Ryna's Gulch, Shalimar, Virginia.

He closed his eyes and thought of the black men in Shalimar, Roanoke, Petersburg, Newport News, Danville, in the Blood Bank, on Darling Street, in the pool halls, the barbershops. Their names. Names they got from yearnings, gestures, flaws, events, mistakes, weaknesses. Names that bore witness. Macon Dead, Sing Byrd, Crowell Byrd, Pilate, Reba, Hagar, Magdalene, First Corinthians, Milkman, Guitar, Railroad Tommy, Hospital Tommy, Empire State (he just stood around and swayed), Small Boy, Sweet, Circe, Moon, Nero, Humpty-Dumpty, Blue Boy, Scandinavia, Quack-Quack, Jericho, Spoonbread, Ice Man, Dough Belly, Rocky River, Gray Eye, Cock-a-Doodle-Doo, Cool Breeze, Muddy Waters, Pinetop, Jelly Roll, Fats, Lead-belly, Bo Diddley, Cat-Iron, Peg-Leg, Son, Shortstuff, Smoky Babe, Funny Papa, Bukka, Pink, Bull Moose, B. B., T-Bone, Black Ace, Lemon, Washboard, Gatemouth, Cleanhead, Tampa Red, Juke Boy, Shine, Staggerlee, Jim the Devil, Fuck-Up, and *Dat* Nigger.

Angling out from these thoughts of names was one

more – the one that whispered in the spinning wheels of the bus: 'Guitar is biding his time. Guitar is biding his time. Your day has come. Your day has come. Guitar is biding his time. Guitar is a very good Day. Guitar is a very good Day. A very good Day, a very good Day, and biding, biding his time.'

In the seventy-five-dollar car, and here on the big Greyhound, Milkman felt safe. But there were days and days ahead. Maybe if Guitar was back in the city now, among familiar surroundings, Milkman could defuse him. And certainly, in time, he would discover his foolishness. There was no gold. And although things would never be the same between them, at least the man-hunt would be over.

Even as he phrased the thought in his mind, Milkman knew it was not so. Either Guitar's disappointment with the gold that was not there was so deep it had deranged him, or his 'work' had done it. Or maybe he simply allowed himself to feel about Milkman what he had always felt about Macon Dead and the Honoré crowd. In any case, he had snatched the first straw, limp and wet as it was, to prove to himself the need to kill Milkman. The Sunday-school girls deserved better than to be avenged by that hawk-headed raven-skinned Sunday man who included in his blood sweep four innocent white girls and one innocent black man.

Perhaps that's what all human relationships boiled down to: Would you save my life? or would you take it?

'Everybody wants a black man's life.'

Yeah. And black men were not excluded. With two exceptions, everybody he was close to seemed to prefer him out of this life. And the two exceptions were both women, both black, both old. From the beginning, his mother and Pilate had fought for his life, and he had never so much as made either of them a cup of tea.

Would you save my life or would you take it? Guitar was exceptional. To both questions he could answer yes.

From the novel *The Bluest Eye*

1.

SHE SLEPT IN the bed with us. Frieda on the outside because she is brave – it never occurs to her that if in her sleep her hand hangs over the edge of the bed 'something' will crawl out from under it and bite her fingers off. I sleep near the wall because that thought *has* occurred to me. Pecola, therefore, had to sleep in the middle.

Mama had told us two days earlier that a 'case' was coming – a girl who had no place to go. The county had placed her in our house for a few days until they could decide what to do, or, more precisely, until the family was reunited. We were to be nice to her and not fight. Mama didn't know 'what got into people,' but that old Dog Breedlove had burned up his house, gone upside his wife's head, and everybody, as a result, was outdoors.

Outdoors, we knew, was the real terror of life. The threat of being outdoors surfaced frequently in those days. Every possibility of excess was curtailed with it. If somebody ate too much, he could end up outdoors. If somebody used too much coal, he could end up outdoors. People could gamble themselves outdoors, drink themselves outdoors. Sometimes mothers put their sons outdoors, and when that happened, regardless of what the son had done, all sympathy was with him. He was outdoors, and his own flesh had done it. To be put outdoors by a landlord was one thing – unfortunate, but an aspect of life over which you had no control, since you could not control your income. But to be slack enough to put oneself outdoors, or heartless enough to put one's own kin outdoors – that was criminal.

There is a difference between being put *out* and being put out*doors.* If you are put out, you go somewhere else; if you are outdoors, there is no place to go. The distinction was subtle but final. Outdoors was the end of something, an irrevocable, physical fact, defining and complementing our metaphysical condition. Being a minority in both caste and class, we moved about anyway on the hem of life, struggling to consolidate our weaknesses and hang on, or to creep singly up into the major folds of the garment. Our peripheral existence, however, was something we had learned to deal with – probably because it was abstract. But the concreteness of being outdoors was another matter – like the difference between the concept of death and being, in fact, dead. Dead doesn't change, and outdoors is here to stay.

Knowing that there was such a thing as outdoors bred

in us a hunger for property, for ownership. The firm possession of a yard, a porch, a grape arbor. Propertied black people spent all their energies, all their love, on their nests. Like frenzied, desperate birds, they overdecorated everything; fussed and fidgeted over their hard-won homes; canned, jellied, and preserved all summer to fill the cupboards and shelves; they painted, picked, and poked at every corner of their houses. And these houses loomed like hothouse sunflowers among the rows of weeds that were the rented houses. Renting blacks cast furtive glances at these owned yards and porches, and made firmer commitments to buy themselves 'some nice little old place.' In the meantime, they saved, and scratched, and piled away what they could in the rented hovels, looking forward to the day of property.

Cholly Breedlove, then, a renting black, having put his family outdoors, had catapulted himself beyond the reaches of human consideration. He had joined the animals; was, indeed, an old dog, a snake, a ratty nigger. Mrs Breedlove was staying with the woman she worked for; the boy, Sammy, was with some other family; and Pecola was to stay with us. Cholly was in jail.

She came with nothing. No little paper bag with the other dress, or a nightgown, or two pair of whitish cotton bloomers. She just appeared with a white woman and sat down.

We had fun in those few days Pecola was with us. Frieda and I stopped fighting each other and concentrated on our guest, trying hard to keep her from feeling outdoors.

When we discovered that she clearly did not want to dominate us, we liked her. She laughed when I clowned for her, and smiled and accepted gracefully the food gifts my sister gave her.

'Would you like some graham crackers?'

'I don't care.'

Frieda brought her four graham crackers on a saucer and some milk in a blue-and-white Shirley Temple cup. She was a long time with the milk, and gazed fondly at the silhouette of Shirley Temple's dimpled face. Frieda and she had a loving conversation about how cu-ute Shirley Temple was. I couldn't join them in their adoration because I hated Shirley. Not because she was cute, but because she danced with Bojangles, who was *my* friend, *my* uncle, *my* daddy, and who ought to have been soft-shoeing it and chuckling with me. Instead he was enjoying, sharing, giving a lovely dance thing with one of those little white girls whose socks never slid down under their heels. So I said, 'I like Jane Withers.'

They gave me a puzzled look, decided I was incomprehensible, and continued their reminiscing about old squint-eyed Shirley.

Younger than both Frieda and Pecola, I had not yet arrived at the turning point in the development of my psyche which would allow me to love her. What I felt at that time was unsullied hatred. But before that I had felt a stranger, more frightening thing than hatred for all the Shirley Temples of the world.

It had begun with Christmas and the gift of dolls. The big, the special, the loving gift was always a big, blue-eyed Baby Doll. From the clucking sounds of adults I knew that the doll represented what they thought was my fondest wish. I was bemused with the thing itself, and the way it looked. What was I supposed to do with it? Pretend I was its mother? I had no interest in babies or the concept of motherhood. I was interested only in humans my own age and size, and could not generate any enthusiasm at the prospect of being a mother. Motherhood was old age, and other remote possibilities. I learned quickly, however, what I was expected to do with the doll: rock it, fabricate storied situations around it, even sleep with it. Picture books were full of little girls sleeping with their dolls. Raggedy Ann dolls usually, but they were out of the question. I was physically revolted by and secretly frightened of those round moronic eyes, the pancake face, and orangeworms hair.

The other dolls, which were supposed to bring me great pleasure, succeeded in doing quite the opposite. When I took it to bed, its hard unyielding limbs resisted my flesh – the tapered fingertips on those dimpled hands scratched. If, in sleep, I turned, the bone-cold head collided with my own. It was a most uncomfortable, patently aggressive sleeping companion. To hold it was no more rewarding. The starched gauze or lace on the cotton dress irritated any embrace. I had only one desire: to dismember it. To see of what it was made, to discover the dearness, to find the beauty, the desirability that had escaped me, but apparently only me. Adults, older girls, shops, magazines, newspapers, window signs – all the world had agreed that a blue-eyed, yellow-haired, pink-skinned doll was what every girl child treasured. 'Here,' they said, 'this is beautiful, and if you are on this day "worthy" you may have it.' I fingered the face, wondering at the single-stroke eyebrows; picked at the pearly teeth stuck like two piano keys between red bowline lips. Traced the turned-up nose, poked the glassy blue eyeballs, twisted the yellow hair. I could not love it. But I could examine it to see what it was that all the world said was lovable. Break off the tiny fingers, bend the flat feet, loosen the hair, twist the head around, and the thing made one sound – a sound they said was the sweet and plaintive cry 'Mama,' but which sounded to me like the bleat of a dying lamb, or, more precisely, our icebox door opening on rusty hinges in July. Remove the cold and stupid eyeball, it would bleat still, 'Ahhhhhh,' take off the head, shake out the sawdust, crack the back against the brass bed rail, it would bleat still. The gauze back would split, and I could see the disk with six holes, the secret of the sound. A mere metal roundness.

Grown people frowned and fussed: 'You-don't-know-how-to-take-care-of-nothing. I-never-had-a-baby-doll-in-my-whole-life-and-used-to-cry-my-eyes-out-for-them. Now-you-got-one-a-beautiful-one-and-you-tear-it-up-what's-the-matter-with-you?'

How strong was their outrage. Tears threatened to erase the aloofness of their authority. The emotion of years of unfulfilled longing preened in their voices. I did not know why I destroyed those dolls. But I did know that nobody ever asked me what I wanted for Christmas. Had any adult with the power to fulfill my desires taken me seriously and asked me what I wanted, they would have known that I did not want to have anything to own, or to possess any object. I wanted rather to feel something on Christmas day. The real question would have been, 'Dear Claudia, what experience would you like on Christmas?' I could have spoken up, 'I want to sit on the low stool in Big Mama's kitchen with my lap full of lilacs and listen to Big Papa play his violin for me alone.' The lowness of the stool made for my body, the security and warmth of Big Mama's kitchen, the smell of the lilacs, the sound of the music, and, since it would be good to have all of my senses engaged, the taste of a peach, perhaps, afterward.

Instead I tasted and smelled the acridness of tin plates and cups designed for tea parties that bored me. Instead I looked with loathing on new dresses that required a hateful bath in a galvanized zinc tub before wearing. Slipping around on the zinc, no time to play or soak, for the water chilled too fast, no time to enjoy one's nakedness, only time to make curtains of soapy water carcen down between the legs. Then the scratchy towels and the dreadful and humiliating absence of dirt. The irritable, unimaginative cleanliness. Gone the ink marks from legs and face, all my creations and accumulations of the day gone, and replaced by goose pimples.

I destroyed white baby dolls.

But the dismembering of dolls was not the true horror. The truly horrifying thing was the transference of the same impulses to little white girls. The indifference with which I could have axed them was shaken only by my desire to do so. To discover what eluded me: the secret of the magic they weaved on others. What made people look at them and say, 'Awwwww,' but not for me? The eye slide of black women as they approached them on the street, and the possessive gentleness of their touch as they handled them.

If I pinched them, their eyes – unlike the crazed glint of the baby doll's eyes – would fold in pain, and their cry would not be the sound of an icebox door, but a fascinating cry of pain. When I learned how repulsive this disinterested violence was, that it was repulsive because it was disinterested, my shame floundered about for refuge. The best hiding place was love. Thus the conversion from pristine sadism to fabricated hatred, to fraudulent love. It was a small step to Shirley Temple. I learned much later to worship her, just as I learned to delight in cleanliness, knowing, even as I learned, that the change was adjustment without improvement.

LETTING HERSELF BREATHE easy now, Pecola covered her head with the quilt. The sick feeling, which she had tried to prevent by holding in her stomach, came quickly in spite of her precaution. There surged in her the desire to heave, but as always, she knew she would not.

'Please, God,' she whispered into the palm of her hand. 'Please make me disappear.' She squeezed her eyes shut. Little parts of her body faded away. Now slowly, now with a rush. Slowly again. Her fingers went, one by one; then her arms disappeared all the way to the elbow. Her feet now. Yes, that was good. The legs all at once. It was hardest above the thighs. She had to be real still and pull. Her stomach would not go. But finally it, too, went away. Then her chest, her neck. The face was hard, too. Almost done, almost. Only her tight, tight eyes were left. They were always left.

Try as she might, she could never get her eyes to disappear. So what was the point? They were everything. Everything was there, in them. All of those pictures, all of those faces. She had long ago given up the idea of running away to see new pictures, new faces, as Sammy had so often done. He never took her, and he never thought about his going ahead of time, so it was never planned. It wouldn't have worked anyway. As long as she looked the way she did, as long as she was ugly, she would have to stay with these people. Somehow she belonged to them. Long hours she sat looking in the mirror, trying to discover the secret of the ugliness, the ugliness that made her ignored or despised at school, by teachers and classmates alike. She was the only member of her class who sat alone at a double desk. The first letter of her last name forced her to sit in the front of the room always. But what about Marie Appolonaire? Marie was in front of her, but she shared a desk with Luke Angelino. Her teachers had always treated her this way. They tried never to glance at her, and called on her only when everyone was required to respond. She also knew that when one of the girls at school wanted to be particularly insulting to a boy, or wanted to get an immediate response from him, she could say. 'Bobby loves Pecola Breedlove! Bobby loves Pecola Breedlove!' and never fail to get peals of laughter from those in earshot, and mock anger from the accused.

It had occurred to Pecola some time ago that if her eyes, those eyes that held the pictures, and knew the sights – if those eyes of hers were different, that is to say, beautiful, she herself would be different. Her teeth were good, and at least her nose was not big and flat like some of those who were thought so cute. If she looked different, beautiful, maybe Cholly would be different, and Mrs Breedlove too. Maybe they'd say, 'Why, look at pretty-eyed Pecola. We mustn't do bad things in front of those pretty eyes.'

Pretty eyes. Pretty blue eyes. Big blue pretty eyes.
Run, Jip, run. Jip runs, Alice runs. Alice has blue eyes.
Jerry has blue eyes. Jerry runs. Alice runs. They run
with their blue eyes. Four blue eyes. Four pretty
blue eyes. Blue-sky eyes. Blue-like Mrs Forrest's

blue blouse eyes. Morning-glory-blue-eyes.
Alice-and-Jerry-blue-storybook-eyes.

Each night, without fail, she prayed for blue eyes. Fervently, for a year she had prayed. Although somewhat discouraged, she was not without hope. To have something as wonderful as that happen would take a long, long time.

Thrown, in this way, into the binding conviction that only a miracle could relieve her, she would never know her beauty. She would see only what there was to see: the eyes of other people.

She walks down Garden Avenue to a small grocery store which sells penny candy. Three pennies are in her shoe – slipping back and forth between the sock and the inner sole. With each step she feels the painful press of the coins against her foot. A sweet, endurable, even cherished irritation, full of promise and delicate security. There is plenty of time to consider what to buy. Now, however, she moves down an avenue gently buffeted by the familiar and therefore loved images. The dandelions at the base of the telephone pole. Why, she wonders, do people call them weeds? She thought they were pretty. But grown-ups say, 'Miss Dunion keeps her yard so nice. Not a dandelion anywhere.' Hunkie women in black babushkas go into the fields with baskets to pull them up. But they do not want the yellow heads – only the jagged leaves. They make dandelion soup. Dandelion wine.

Nobody loves the head of a dandelion. Maybe because they are so many, strong, and soon.

There was the sidewalk crack shaped like a Y, and the other one that lifted the concrete up from the dirt floor. Frequently her sloughing step had made her trip over that one. Skates would go well over this sidewalk – old it was, and smooth; it made the wheels glide evenly, with a mild whirr. The newly paved walks were bumpy and uncomfortable, and the sound of skate wheels on new walks was grating.

These and other inanimate things she saw and experienced. They were real to her. She knew them. They were the codes and touchstones of the world, capable of translation and possession. She owned the crack that made her stumble; she owned the clumps of dandelions whose white heads, last fall, she had blown away; whose yellow heads, this fall, she peered into. And owning them made her part of the world, and the world a part of her.

She climbs four wooden steps to the door of Yacobowski's Fresh Veg. Meat and Sundries Store. A bell tinkles as she opens it. Standing before the counter, she looks at the array of candies. All Mary Janes, she decides. Three for a penny. The resistant sweetness that breaks open at last to deliver peanut butter – the oil and salt which complement the sweet pull of caramel. A peal of anticipation unsettles her stomach.

She pulls off her shoe and takes out the three pennies. The gray head of Mr Yacobowski looms up over the counter. He urges his eyes out of his thoughts to encounter her. Blue eyes. Blear-dropped. Slowly, like Indian summer moving imperceptibly toward fall, he looks toward her. Somewhere between retina and object, between vision and view, his eyes draw back, hesitate, and hover. At some fixed point in time and space he senses that he need not waste the effort of a glance. He does not see her, because for him there is nothing to see. How can a fifty-two-year-old white immigrant storekeeper with the taste of potatoes and beer in his mouth, his mind honed on the doe-eyed Virgin Mary, his sensibilities blunted by a permanent awareness of loss, *see* a little black girl? Nothing in his life even suggested that the feat was possible, not to say desirable or necessary.

'Yeah?'

She looks up at him and sees the vacuum where curiosity ought to lodge. And something more. The total absence of human recognition – the glazed separateness. She does not know what keeps his glance suspended. Perhaps because he is grown, or a man, and she a little girl. But she has seen interest, disgust, even anger in grown male eyes. Yet this vacuum is not new to her. It has an edge; somewhere in the bottom lid is the distaste. She has seen it lurking in the eyes of all white people. So. The distaste must be for her, her blackness. All things in her are flux and anticipation. But her blackness is static and dread. And it is the blackness that accounts for, that creates, the vacuum edged with distaste in white eyes.

He does not see her, because for him there is nothing to see

She points her finger at the Mary Janes – a little black shaft of finger, its tip pressed on the display window. The quietly inoffensive assertion of a black child's attempt to communicate with a white adult.

'Them.' The word is more sigh than sense.

'What? These? These?' Phlegm and impatience mingle in his voice.

She shakes her head, her fingertip fixed on the spot which, in her view, at any rate, identifies the Mary Janes. He cannot see her view – the angle of his vision, the slant of her finger, makes it incomprehensible to him. His lumpy red hand plops around in the glass casing like the agitated head of a chicken outraged by the loss of its body.

'Christ. Kantcha talk?'

His fingers brush the Mary Janes.

She nods.

'Well, why'nt you say so? One? How many?'

Pecola unfolds her fist, showing the three pennies. He scoots three Mary Janes toward her   three yellow rectangles in each packet. She holds the money toward him. He hesitates, not wanting to touch her hand. She does not know how to move the finger of her right hand from the display counter or how to get the coins out of her left hand. Finally he reaches over and takes the pennies from her hand. His nails graze her damp palm.

Outside, Pecola feels the inexplicable shame ebb.

Dandelions. A dart of affection leaps out from her to them. But they do not look at her and do not send love back. She thinks, 'They *are* ugly. They *are* weeds.' Pre-occupied with that revelation, she trips on the sidewalk crack. Anger stirs and wakes in her; it opens its mouth, and like a hot-mouthed puppy, laps up the dredges of her shame.

Anger is better. There is a sense of being in anger. A reality and presence. An awareness of worth. It is a lovely surging. Her thoughts fall back to Mr Yacobowski's eyes, his phlegmy voice. The anger will not hold; the puppy is too easily surfeited. Its thirst too quickly quenched, it sleeps. The shame wells up again, its muddy rivulets seeping into her eyes. What to do before the tears come. She remembers the Mary Janes.

Each pale yellow wrapper has a picture on it. A picture of little Mary Jane, for whom the candy is named. Smiling white face. Blond hair in gentle disarray, blue eyes looking at her out of a world of clean comfort. The eyes are petu-lant, mischievous. To Pecola they are simply pretty. She eats the candy, and its sweetness is good. To eat the candy is somehow to eat the eyes, eat Mary Jane. Love Mary Jane. Be Mary Jane.

Three pennies had bought her nine lovely orgasms with Mary Jane. Lovely Mary Jane, for whom a candy is named.

2.

THEY COME FROM Mobile. Aiken. From Newport News. From Marietta. From Meridian. And the sound of these places in their mouths make you think of love. When you ask them where they are from, they tilt their heads and say 'Mobile' and you think you've been kissed. They say 'Aiken' and you see a white butterfly glance off a fence with a torn wing. They say 'Nagadoches' and you want to say 'Yes, I will.' You don't know what these towns are like, but you love what happens to the air when they open their lips and let the names ease out.

Meridian. The sound of it opens the windows of a room like the first four notes of a hymn. Few people can say the names of their home towns with such sly affection. Perhaps because they don't have home towns, just places where they were born. But these girls soak up the juice of their home towns, and it never leaves them. They are thin brown girls who have looked long at hollyhocks in the backyards of Meridian, Mobile, Aiken, and Baton Rouge. And like hollyhocks they are narrow, tall, and still. Their roots are deep, their stalks are firm, and only the top blossom nods in the wind. They have the eyes of people who can tell what time it is by the color of the sky. Such girls live in quiet black neighborhoods where everybody is gainfully employed. Where there are porch swings hanging from chains. Where the grass is cut with a scythe, where rooster combs and sunflowers grow in the yards, and pots of bleeding heart, ivy, and mother-in-law tongue line the steps and windowsills. Such girls have bought watermelon and snapbeans from the fruit man's wagon. They have put in the window the cardboard sign that has a pound measure printed on each of three edges – 10 lbs., 25 lbs., 50 lbs. – and NO ICE on the fourth. These particular brown girls from Mobile and Aiken are not like some of their sisters. They are not fretful, nervous, or shrill; they do not have lovely black necks that stretch as though against an invisible collar; their eyes do not bite. These sugar-brown Mobile girls move through the streets without a stir. They are as sweet and plain as butter-cake. Slim ankles; long, narrow feet. They wash themselves with orange-colored Lifebuoy soap, dust themselves with Cashmere Bouquet talc, clean their teeth with salt on a piece of rag, soften their skin with Jergens Lotion. They smell like wood, newspapers, and vanilla. They straighten their hair with Dixie Peach, and part it on the side. At night they curl it in paper from brown bags, tie a print scarf around their heads, and sleep with hands folded across their stomachs. They do not drink, smoke, or swear, and they still call sex 'nookey.' They sing second soprano in the choir, and although their voices are clear and steady, they are never picked to solo. They are in the second row, white blouses starched, blue skirts almost purple from ironing.

They go to land-grant colleges, normal schools, and learn how to do the white man's work with refinement: home economics to prepare his food; teacher education to instruct black children in obedience; music to soothe the weary master and entertain his blunted soul. Here they learn the rest of the lesson begun in those soft houses with porch swings and pots of bleeding heart: how to behave. The careful development of thrift, patience, high morals, and good manners. In short, how to get rid of the funkiness. The dreadful funkiness of passion, the funkiness of nature, the funkiness of the wide range of human emotions.

Wherever it erupts, this Funk, they wipe it away; where it crusts, they dissolve it; wherever it drips, flowers, or clings, they find it and fight it until it dies. They fight this battle all the way to the grave. The laugh that is a little too loud; the enunciation a little too round; the gesture a little too generous. They hold their behind in for fear of a sway too free; when they wear lipstick, they never cover the entire mouth for fear of lips too thick, and they worry, worry, worry about the edges of their hair.

They never seem to have boyfriends, but they always marry. Certain men watch them, without seeming to, and know that if such a girl is in his house, he will sleep on sheets boiled white, hung out to dry on juniper bushes, and pressed flat with a heavy iron. There will be pretty paper flowers decorating the picture of his mother, a large Bible in the front room. They feel secure. They know their work clothes will be mended, washed, and ironed on Monday, that their Sunday shirts will billow on hangers from the door jamb, stiffly starched and white. They look at her hands and know what she will do with biscuit dough; they smell the coffee and the fried ham; see the white, smoky grits with a dollop of butter on top. Her hips assure them that she will bear children easily and painlessly. And they are right.

What they do not know is that this plain brown girl will build her nest stick by stick, make it her own inviolable world, and stand guard over its every plant, weed, and doily, even against him. In silence will she return the lamp to where she put it in the first place; remove the dishes from the table as soon as the last bite is taken; wipe the doorknob after a greasy hand has touched it. A sidelong look will be enough to tell him to smoke on the back porch. Children will sense instantly that they cannot come into her yard to retrieve a ball. But the men do not know these things. Nor do they know that she will give him her body sparingly and partially. He must enter her surreptitiously, lifting the hem of her nightgown only to her navel. He must rest his weight on his elbows when they make love, ostensibly to avoid hurting her breasts but actually to keep her from having to touch or feel too much of him.

While he moves inside her, she will wonder why they didn't put the necessary but private parts of the body in some more convenient place – like the armpit, for example, or the palm of the hand. Someplace one could get to easily, and quickly, without undressing. She stiffens when she feels one of her paper curlers coming undone from the activity of love; imprints in her mind which one it is that is coming loose so she can quickly secure it once he is through. She hopes he will not sweat – the damp may get into her hair; and that she will remain dry between her legs – she hates the glucking sound they make when she is moist. When she senses some spasm about to grip him, she will make rapid movements with her hips, press her fingernails into his back, suck in her breath, and pretend she is having an orgasm. She might wonder again, for the six hundredth time, what it would be like to have *that* feeling while her husband's penis is inside her. The closest thing to it was the time she was walking down the street and her napkin slipped free of her sanitary belt. It moved gently between her legs as she walked. Gently, ever so gently. And then a slight and distinctly delicious sensation collected in her crotch. As the delight grew, she had to stop in the street, hold her thighs together to contain it. That must be what it is like, she thinks, but it never happens while he is inside her. When he withdraws, she pulls her nightgown down, slips out of the bed and into the bathroom with relief.

Occasionally some living thing will engage her affections. A cat, perhaps, who will love her order, precision, and constancy; who will be as clean and quiet as she is. The cat will settle quietly on the windowsill and caress her with his eyes. She can hold him in her arms, letting his back paws struggle for footing on her breast and his fore-paws cling to her shoulder. She can rub the smooth fur and feel the unresisting flesh underneath. At her gentlest touch he will preen, stretch, and open his mouth. And she will accept the strangely pleasant sensation that comes when he writhes beneath her hand and flattens his eyes with a surfeit of sensual delight. When she stands cooking at the table, he will circle about her shanks, and the trill of his fur spirals up her legs to her thighs, to make her fingers tremble a little in the pie dough.

Or, as she sits reading the 'Uplifting Thoughts' in *The Liberty Magazine*, the cat will jump into her lap. She will fondle that soft hill of hair and let the warmth of the animal's body seep over and into the deeply private areas of her lap. Sometimes the magazine drops, and she opens her legs just a little, and the two of them will be still together, perhaps shifting a little together, sleeping a little together, until four o'clock, when the intruder comes home from work vaguely anxious about what's for dinner.

The cat will always know that he is first in her affections. Even after she bears a child. For she does bear a child – easily, and painlessly. But only one. A son. Named Junior.

One such girl from Mobile, or Meridian, or Aiken who did not sweat in her armpits nor between her thighs, who smelled of wood and vanilla, who had made soufflés in the Home Economics Department, moved with her husband, Louis, to Lorain, Ohio. Her name was Geraldine. There she built her nest, ironed shirts, potted bleeding hearts, played with her cat, and birthed Louis Junior.

Geraldine did not allow her baby, Junior, to cry. As long as his needs were physical, she could meet them – comfort and satiety. He was always brushed, bathed, oiled, and shod. Geraldine did not talk to him, coo to him, or indulge him in kissing bouts, but she saw that every other desire was fulfilled. It was not long before the child discovered the difference in his mother's behavior to himself and the cat. As he grew older, he learned how to direct his hatred of his mother to the cat, and spent some happy moments watching it suffer. The cat survived, because Geraldine was seldom away from home, and could effectively soothe the animal when Junior abused him.

Geraldine, Louis, Junior, and the cat lived next to the playground of Washington Irving School. Junior considered the playground his own, and the schoolchildren coveted his freedom to sleep late, go home for lunch, and dominate the playground after school. He hated to see the swings, slides, monkey bars, and seesaws empty and tried to get kids to stick around as long as possible. White kids; his mother did not like him to play with niggers. She had explained to him the difference between colored people and niggers. They were easily identifiable. Colored people were neat and quiet; niggers were dirty and loud. He belonged to the former group: he wore white shirts and blue trousers; his hair was cut as close to his scalp as possible to avoid any suggestion of wool, the part was etched into his hair by the barber. In winter his mother put Jergens Lotion on his face to keep the skin from becoming ashen. Even though he was light-skinned, it was possible to ash. The line between colored and nigger was not always clear; subtle and telltale signs threatened to erode it, and the watch had to be constant.

Junior used to long to play with the black boys. More than anything in the world he wanted to play King of the Mountain and have them push him down the mound of dirt and roll over him. He wanted to feel their hardness pressing on him, smell their wild blackness, and say 'Fuck you' with that lovely casualness. He wanted to sit with them on curbstones and compare the sharpness of jackknives, the distance and arcs of spitting. In the toilet he wanted to share with them the laurels of being able to pee far and long. Bay Boy and P. L. had at one time been his idols. Gradually he came to agree with his mother that neither Bay Boy nor P. L. was good enough for him. He played only with Ralph Nisensky, who was two years younger, wore glasses, and didn't want to *do* anything. More and more Junior enjoyed bullying girls. It was easy making them scream and run. How he laughed when they fell down and their bloomers showed. When they got up, their faces red and crinkled, it made him feel good. The nigger girls he did not pick on very much. They usually traveled in packs, and once when he threw a stone at some of them, they chased, caught, and beat him witless. He lied to his mother, saying Bay Boy did it. His mother was very upset. His father just kept on reading the Lorain *Journal*.

When the mood struck him, he would call a child passing by to come play on the swings or the seesaw. If the child wouldn't, or did and left too soon, Junior threw gravel at him. He became a very good shot.

Alternately bored and frightened at home, the playground was his joy. On a day when he had been especially idle, he saw a very black girl taking a shortcut through the playground. She kept her head down as she walked. He had seen her many times before, standing alone, always alone, at recess. Nobody ever played with her. Probably, he thought, because she was ugly.

Now Junior called to her. 'Hey! What are you doing walking through my yard?'

The girl stopped.

'Nobody can come through this yard 'less I say so.'

'This ain't your yard. It's the school's.'

'But I'm in charge of it.'

The girl started to walk away.

'Wait.' Junior walked toward her. 'You can play in it if you want to. What's your name?'

'Pecola. I don't want to play.'

'Come on. I'm not going to bother you.'

'I got to go home.'

'Say, you want to see something? I got something to show you.'

'No. What is it?'

'Come on in my house. See, I live right there. Come on. I'll show you.'

'Show me what?'

'Some kittens. We got some kittens. You can have one if you want.'

'Real kittens?'

'Yeah. Come on.'

He pulled gently at her dress. Pecola began to move toward his house. When he knew she had agreed, Junior ran ahead excitedly, stopping only to yell back at her to come on. He held the door open for her, smiling his encouragement. Pecola climbed the porch stairs and hesitated there, afraid to follow him. The house looked dark. Junior said, 'There's nobody here. My ma's gone out, and my father's at work. Don't you want to see the kittens?'

Junior turned on the lights. Pecola stepped inside the door.

How beautiful, she thought. What a beautiful house. There was a big red-and-gold Bible on the dining-room table. Little lace doilies were everywhere – on arms and backs of chairs, in the center of a large dining table, on little tables. Potted plants were on all the windowsills. A color picture of Jesus Christ hung on a wall with the prettiest paper flowers fastened on the frame. She wanted to see everything slowly, slowly. But Junior kept saying, 'Hey, you. Come on. Come on.' He pulled her into another room, even more beautiful than the first. More doilies, a big lamp with green-and-gold base and white shade. There was even a rug on the floor, with enormous dark-red flowers. She was deep in admiration of the flowers when Junior said, 'Here!' Pecola turned. 'Here is your kitten!' he screeched. And he threw a big black cat right in her face. She sucked in her breath in fear and surprise and felt fur in her mouth. The cat clawed her face and chest in an effort to right itself, then leaped nimbly to the floor.

Junior was laughing and running around the room clutching his stomach delightedly. Pecola touched the scratched place on her face and felt tears coming. When she started toward the doorway, Junior leaped in front of her.

'You can't get out. You're my prisoner,' he said. His eyes were merry but hard.

'You let me go.'

'No!' He pushed her down, ran out the door that separated the rooms, and held it shut with his hands. Pecola's banging on the door increased his gasping, high-pitched laughter.

The tears came fast, and she held her face in her hands. When something soft and furry moved around her ankles, she jumped, and saw it was the cat. He wound himself in and about her legs. Momentarily distracted from her fear, she squatted down to touch him, her hands wet from the tears. The cat rubbed up against her knee. He was black all over, deep silky black, and his eyes, pointing down toward his nose, were bluish green. The light made them shine like blue ice. Pecola rubbed the cat's head; he whined, his tongue flicking with pleasure. The blue eyes in the black face held her.

Junior, curious at not hearing her sobs, opened the door, and saw her squatting down rubbing the cat's back. He saw the cat stretching its head and flattening its eyes. He had seen that expression many times as the animal responded to his mother's touch.

'Gimme my cat!' His voice broke. With a movement both awkward and sure he snatched the cat by one of its hind legs and began to swing it around his head in a circle.

'Stop that!' Pecola was screaming. The cat's free paws were stiffened, ready to grab anything to restore balance, its mouth wide, its eyes blue streaks of horror.

Still screaming, Pecola reached for Junior's hand. She heard her dress rip under her arm. Junior tried to push her away, but she grabbed the arm which was swinging the cat. They both fell, and in falling, Junior let go the cat, which, having been released in mid-motion, was thrown full force against the window. It slithered down and fell on the radiator behind the sofa. Except for a few shudders, it was still. There was only the slightest smell of singed fur.

Geraldine opened the door.

'What is this?' Her voice was mild, as though asking a perfectly reasonable question. 'Who is this girl?'

'She killed our cat,' said Junior. 'Look.' He pointed to the radiator, where the cat lay, its blue eyes closed, leaving only an empty, black, and helpless face.

Geraldine went to the radiator and picked up the cat. He was limp in her arms, but she rubbed her face in his fur. She looked at Pecola. Saw the dirty torn dress, the plaits sticking out on her head, hair matted where the plaits had come undone, the muddy shoes with the wad of gum peeping out from between the cheap soles, the soiled socks, one of which had been walked down into the heel of the shoe. She saw the safety pin holding the hem of the dress up. Up over the hump of the cat's back she looked at her. She had seen this little girl all of her life. Hanging out of windows over saloons in Mobile, crawling over the porches of shotgun houses on the edge of town, sitting in bus stations holding paper bags and crying to mothers who kept saying 'Shet up!' Hair uncombed, dresses falling apart, shoes untied and caked with dirt. They had stared at her with great uncomprehending eyes. Eyes that questioned nothing and asked everything. Unblinking and unabashed, they stared up at her. The end of the world lay in their eyes, and the beginning, and all the waste in between.

They were everywhere. They slept six in a bed, all their pee mixing together in the night as they wet their beds each in his own candy-and-potato-chip dream. In the long, hot days, they idled away, picking plaster from the walls and digging into the earth with sticks. They sat in little rows on street curbs, crowded into pews at church, taking space from the nice, neat, colored children; they clowned on the playgrounds, broke things in dime stores, ran in front of you on the street, made ice slides on the sloped sidewalks in winter. The girls grew up knowing nothing of girdles, and the boys announced their manhood by turning the bills of their caps backward. Grass wouldn't grow where they lived. Flowers died. Shades fell down. Tin cans and tires blossomed where they lived. They lived on cold black-eyed peas and orange pop. Like flies they hovered; like flies they settled. And this one had settled in her house. Up over the hump of the cat's back she looked.

'Get out,' she said, her voice quiet. 'You nasty little black bitch. Get out of my house.'

The cat shuddered and flicked his tail.

Pecola backed out of the room, staring at the pretty milk-brown lady in the pretty gold-and-green house who was talking to her through the cat's fur. The pretty lady's words made the cat fur move; the breath of each word parted the fur. Pecola turned to find the front door and saw Jesus looking down at her with sad and unsurprised eyes, his long brown hair parted in the middle, the gay paper flowers twisted around his face.

Outside, the March wind blew into the rip in her dress. She held her head down against the cold. But she could not hold it low enough to avoid seeing the snowflakes falling and dying on the pavement.

Foreword to *Beloved*

IN 1983 I lost my job – or left it. One, the other, or both. In any case, I had been part-time for a while, coming into the publishing house one day a week to do the correspondence-telephoning-meetings that were part of the job; editing manuscripts at home.

Leaving was a good idea for two reasons. One, I had written four novels and it seemed clear to everyone that writing was my central work. The question of priorities – how can you edit and write at the same time – seemed to me both queer and predictable; it sounded like 'How can you both teach and create?' 'How can a painter or a sculptor or an actor do her work and guide others?' But to many this edit–write combination was conflicting.

The second reason was less ambiguous. The books I had edited were not earning scads of money, even when 'scads' didn't mean what it means now. My list was to me spectacular: writers with outrageous talent (Toni Cade Bambara, June Jordan, Gayle Jones, Lucille Clifton, Henry

Dumas, Leon Forrest); scholars with original ideas and hands-on research (William Hinton's *Shen Fan*, Ivan Van Sertima's *They Came Before Columbus*, Karen DeCrow's *Sexist Justice*, Chinweizu's *The West and the Rest of Us*); public figures eager to set the record straight (Angela Davis, Muhammad Ali, Huey Newton). And when there was a book that I thought needed doing, I found an author to write it. My enthusiasm, shared by some, was muted by others, reflecting the indifferent sales figures. I may be wrong about this, but even in the late seventies, acquiring authors who were certain sellers outranked editing manuscripts or supporting emerging or aging authors through their careers. Suffice it to say, I convinced myself that it was time for me to live like a grown-up writer: off royalties and writing only. I don't know what comic book that notion came from, but I grabbed it.

A few days after my last day at work, sitting in front of my house on the pier jutting out into the Hudson River, I began to feel an edginess instead of the calm I had expected. I ran through my index of problem areas and found nothing new or pressing. I couldn't fathom what was so unexpectedly troubling on a day that perfect, watching a river that serene. I had no agenda and couldn't hear the telephone if it rang. I heard my heart, though, stomping away in my chest like a colt. I went back to the house to examine this apprehension, even panic. I knew what fear felt like; this was different. Then it slapped me: I was happy, free in a way I had never been, ever. It was the

oddest sensation. Not ecstasy, not satisfaction, not a surfeit of pleasure or accomplishment. It was a purer delight,
a rogue anticipation with certainty. Enter *Beloved*.

I think now it was the shock of liberation that drew my
thoughts to what 'free' could possibly mean to women. In
the eighties, the debate was still roiling: equal pay, equal
treatment, access to professions, schools . . . and choice
without stigma. To marry or not. To have children or not.
Inevitably these thoughts led me to the different history of black women in this country – a history in which
marriage was discouraged, impossible, or illegal; in
which birthing children was required, but 'having' them,
being responsible for them – being, in other words, their
parent – was as out of the question as freedom. Assertions
of parenthood under conditions peculiar to the logic of
institutional enslavement were criminal.

The idea was riveting, but the canvas overwhelmed me.
Summoning characters who could manifest the intellect
and the ferocity such logic would provoke proved beyond
my imagination until I remembered one of the books I had
published back when I had a job. A newspaper clipping
in *The Black Book* summarized the story of Margaret Garner, a young mother who, having escaped slavery, was
arrested for killing one of her children (and trying to kill
the others) rather than let them be returned to the
owner's plantation. She became a cause célèbre in the
fight against the Fugitive Slave laws, which mandated
the return of escapees to their owners. Her sanity and

lack of repentance caught the attention of Abolitionists as well as newspapers. She was certainly single-minded and, judging by her comments, she had the intellect, the ferocity, and the willingness to risk everything for what was to her the necessity of freedom.

The historical Margaret Garner is fascinating, but, to a novelist, confining. Too little imaginative space there for my purposes. So I would invent her thoughts, plumb them for a subtext that was historically true in essence, but not strictly factual in order to relate her history to contemporary issues about freedom, responsibility, and women's 'place.' The heroine would represent the unapologetic acceptance of shame and terror; assume the consequences of choosing infanticide; claim her own freedom. The terrain, slavery, was formidable and pathless. To invite readers (and myself) into the repellant landscape (hidden, but not completely; deliberately buried, but not forgotten) was to pitch a tent in a cemetery inhabited by highly vocal ghosts.

I sat on the porch, rocking in a swing, looking at giant stones piled up to take the river's occasional fist. Above the stones is a path through the lawn, but interrupted by an ironwood gazebo situated under a cluster of trees and in deep shade.

She walked out of the water, climbed the rocks, and leaned against the gazebo. Nice hat.

So she was there from the beginning, and except for me, everybody (the characters) knew it – a sentence that later became 'The women in the house knew it.' The figure most central to the story would have to be her, the murdered, not the murderer, the one who lost everything and had no say in any of it. She could not linger outside; she would have to enter the house. A real house, not a cabin. One with an address, one where former slaves lived on their own. There would be no lobby into this house, and there would be no 'introduction' into it or into the novel. I wanted the reader to be kidnapped, thrown ruthlessly into an alien environment as the first step into a shared experience with the book's population – just as the characters were snatched from one place to another, from any place to any other, without preparation or defense.

It was important to name this house, but not the way 'Sweet Home' or other plantations were named. There would be no adjectives suggesting coziness or grandeur or the laying claim to an instant, aristocratic past. Only numbers here to identify the house while simultaneously separating it from a street or city – marking its difference from the houses of other blacks in the neighborhood; allowing it a hint of the superiority, the pride, former slaves would take in having an address of their own. Yet a house that has, literally, a personality – which we call 'haunted' when that personality is blatant.

In trying to make the slave experience intimate, I hoped the sense of things being both under control and out of control would be persuasive throughout; that the order and quietude of everyday life would be violently disrupted by the chaos of the needy dead; that the herculean effort to forget would be threatened by memory desperate to stay alive. To render enslavement as a personal experience, language must get out of the way.

I husband that moment on the pier, the deceptive river, the instant awareness of possibility, the loud heart kicking, the solitude, the danger. And the girl with the nice hat. Then the focus.

From the novel *Beloved*

UNFORTUNATELY HER BRAIN was devious. She might be hurrying across a field, running practically, to get to the pump quickly and rinse the chamomile sap from her legs. Nothing else would be in her mind. The picture of the men coming to nurse her was as lifeless as the nerves in her back where the skin buckled like a washboard. Nor was there the faintest scent of ink or the cherry gum and oak bark from which it was made. Nothing. Just the breeze cooling her face as she rushed toward water. And then sopping the chamomile away with pump water and rags, her mind fixed on getting every last bit of sap off – on her carelessness in taking a shortcut across the field just to save a half mile, and not noticing how high the weeds had grown until the itching was all the way to her knees. Then something. The plash of water, the sight of her shoes and stockings awry on the path where she had flung them; or Here Boy lapping in the puddle near her feet, and suddenly there was Sweet Home rolling,

rolling, rolling out before her eyes, and although there was not a leaf on that farm that did not make her want to scream, it rolled itself out before her in shameless beauty. It never looked as terrible as it was and it made her wonder if hell was a pretty place too. Fire and brimstone all right, but hidden in lacy groves. Boys hanging from the most beautiful sycamores in the world. It shamed her – remembering the wonderful soughing trees rather than the boys. Try as she might to make it otherwise, the sycamores beat out the children every time and she could not forgive her memory for that.

When the last of the chamomile was gone, she went around to the front of the house, collecting her shoes and stockings on the way. As if to punish her further for her terrible memory, sitting on the porch not forty feet away was Paul D, the last of the Sweet Home men. And although she could never mistake his face for another's, she said, 'Is that you?'

'What's left.' He stood up and smiled. 'How you been, girl, besides barefoot?'

When she laughed it came out loose and young. 'Messed up my legs back yonder. Chamomile.'

He made a face as though tasting a teaspoon of something bitter. 'I don't want to even hear 'bout it. Always did hate that stuff.'

Sethe balled up her stockings and jammed them into her pocket. 'Come on in.'

'Porch is fine, Sethe. Cool out here.' He sat back down

and looked at the meadow on the other side of the road, knowing the eagerness he felt would be in his eyes.

'Eighteen years,' she said softly.

'Eighteen,' he repeated. 'And I swear I been walking every one of em. Mind if I join you?' He nodded toward her feet and began unlacing his shoes.

'You want to soak them? Let me get you a basin of water.' She moved closer to him to enter the house.

'No, uh uh. Can't baby feet. A whole lot more tramping they got to do yet.'

'You can't leave right away, Paul D. You got to stay awhile.'

'Well, long enough to see Baby Suggs, anyway. Where is she?'

'Dead.'

'Aw no. When?'

'Eight years now. Almost nine.'

'Was it hard? I hope she didn't die hard.'

Sethe shook her head. 'Soft as cream. Being alive was the hard part. Sorry you missed her though. Is that what you came by for?'

'That's some of what I came for. The rest is you. But if all the truth be known, I go anywhere these days. Anywhere they let me sit down.'

'You looking good.'

'Devil's confusion. He lets me look good long as I feel bad.' He looked at her and the word 'bad' took on another meaning.

Sethe smiled. This is the way they were – had been. All of the Sweet Home men, before and after Halle, treated her to a mild brotherly flirtation, so subtle you had to scratch for it.

Except for a heap more hair and some waiting in his eyes, he looked the way he had in Kentucky. Peachstone skin; straight-backed. For a man with an immobile face it was amazing how ready it was to smile, or blaze or be sorry with you. As though all you had to do was get his attention and right away he produced the feeling you were feeling. With less than a blink, his face seemed to change – underneath it lay the activity.

'I wouldn't have to ask about him, would I? You'd tell me if there was anything to tell, wouldn't you?' Sethe looked down at her feet and saw again the sycamores.

'I'd tell you. Sure I'd tell you. I don't know any more now than I did then.' Except for the churn, he thought, and you don't need to know that. 'You must think he's still alive.'

'No. I think he's dead. It's not being sure that keeps him alive.'

'What did Baby Suggs think?'

'Same, but to listen to her, all her children is dead. Claimed she felt each one go the very day and hour.'

'When she say Halle went?'

'Eighteen fifty-five. The day my baby was born.'

'You had that baby, did you? Never thought you'd make it.' He chuckled. 'Running off pregnant.'

'Had to. Couldn't be no waiting.' She lowered her head and thought, as he did, how unlikely it was that she had made it. And if it hadn't been for that girl looking for velvet, she never would have.

'All by yourself too.' He was proud of her and annoyed by her. Proud she had done it; annoyed that she had not needed Halle or him in the doing.

'Almost by myself. Not all by myself. A whitegirl helped me.'

'Then she helped herself too, God bless her.'

'You could stay the night, Paul D.'

'You don't sound too steady in the offer.'

Sethe glanced beyond his shoulder toward the closed door. 'Oh it's truly meant. I just hope you'll pardon my house. Come on in. Talk to Denver while I cook you something.'

Paul D tied his shoes together, hung them over his shoulder and followed her through the door straight into a pool of red and undulating light that locked him where he stood.

'You got company?' he whispered, frowning.

'Off and on,' said Sethe.

'Good God.' He backed out the door onto the porch. 'What kind of evil you got in here?'

'It's not evil, just sad. Come on. Just step through.'

He looked at her then, closely. Closer than he had when she first rounded the house on wet and shining legs, holding her shoes and stockings up in one hand, her skirts in the other. Halle's girl – the one with iron eyes and back-bone to match. He had never seen her hair in Kentucky. And though her face was eighteen years older than when last he saw her, it was softer now. Because of the hair. A face too still for comfort; irises the same color as her skin, which, in that still face, used to make him think of a mask with mercifully punched-out eyes. Halle's woman. Pregnant every year including the year she sat by the fire telling him she was going to run. Her three children she had already packed into a wagonload of others in a cara-van of Negroes crossing the river. They were to be left with Halle's mother near Cincinnati. Even in that tiny shack, leaning so close to the fire you could smell the heat in her dress, her eyes did not pick up a flicker of light. They were like two wells into which he had trouble gazing. Even punched out they needed to be covered, lidded, marked with some sign to warn folks of what that emptiness held. So he looked instead at the fire while she told him, because her husband was not there for the telling. Mr Garner was dead and his wife had a lump in her neck the size of a sweet potato and unable to speak to anyone. She leaned as close to the fire as her pregnant belly allowed and told him, Paul D, the last of the Sweet Home men.

There had been six of them who belonged to the farm, Sethe the only female. Mrs Garner, crying like a baby, had sold his brother to pay off the debts that surfaced the minute she was widowed. Then schoolteacher arrived to put things in order. But what he did broke three more

Sweet Home men and punched the glittering iron out of Sethe's eyes, leaving two open wells that did not reflect firelight.

Now the iron was back but the face, softened by hair, made him trust her enough to step inside her door smack into a pool of pulsing red light.

She was right. It was sad. Walking through it, a wave of grief soaked him so thoroughly he wanted to cry. It seemed a long way to the normal light surrounding the table, but he made it – dry-eyed and lucky.

'You said she died soft. Soft as cream,' he reminded her.

'That's not Baby Suggs,' she said.

'Who then?'

'My daughter. The one I sent ahead with the boys.'

'She didn't live?'

'No. The one I was carrying when I run away is all I got left. Boys gone too. Both of em walked off just before Baby Suggs died.'

Paul D looked at the spot where the grief had soaked him. The red was gone but a kind of weeping clung to the air where it had been.

Probably best, he thought. If a Negro got legs he ought to use them. Sit down too long, somebody will figure out a way to tie them up. Still . . . if her boys were gone . . .

'No man? You here by yourself?'

'Me and Denver,' she said.

'That all right by you?'

'That's all right by me.'

She saw his skepticism and went on. 'I cook at a restaurant in town. And I sew a little on the sly.'

Paul D smiled then, remembering the bedding dress. Sethe was thirteen when she came to Sweet Home and already iron-eyed. She was a timely present for Mrs Garner who had lost Baby Suggs to her husband's high principles. The five Sweet Home men looked at the new girl and decided to let her be. They were young and so sick with the absence of women they had taken to calves. Yet they let the iron-eyed girl be, so she could choose in spite of the fact that each one would have beaten the others to mush to have her. It took her a year to choose – a long, tough year of thrashing on pallets eaten up with dreams of her. A year of yearning, when rape seemed the solitary gift of life. The restraint they had exercised possible only because they were Sweet Home men – the ones Mr Garner bragged about while other farmers shook their heads in warning at the phrase.

'Y'all got boys,' he told them. 'Young boys, old boys, picky boys, stroppin boys. Now at Sweet Home, my niggers is men every one of em. Bought em thataway, raised em thataway. Men every one.'

'Beg to differ, Garner. Ain't no nigger men.'

'Not if you scared, they ain't.' Garner's smile was wide. 'But if you a man yourself, you'll want your niggers to be men too.'

'I wouldn't have no nigger men round my wife.'

It was the reaction Garner loved and waited for.

'Neither would I,' he said. 'Neither would I,' and there was always a pause before the neighbor, or stranger, or peddler, or brother-in-law or whoever it was got the meaning. Then a fierce argument, sometimes a fight, and Garner came home bruised and pleased, having demonstrated one more time what a real Kentuckian was: one tough enough and smart enough to make and call his own niggers men.

And so they were: Paul D Garner, Paul F Garner, Paul A Garner, Halle Suggs and Sixo, the wild man. All in their twenties, minus women, fucking cows, dreaming of rape, thrashing on pallets, rubbing their thighs and waiting for the new girl – the one who took Baby Suggs' place after Halle bought her with five years of Sundays. Maybe that was why she chose him. A twenty-year-old man so in love with his mother he gave up five years of Sabbaths just to see her sit down for a change was a serious recommendation.

She waited a year. And the Sweet Home men abused cows while they waited with her. She chose Halle and for their first bedding she sewed herself a dress on the sly.

'Won't you stay on awhile? Can't nobody catch up on eighteen years in a day.'

Out of the dimness of the room in which they sat, a white staircase climbed toward the blue-and-white wallpaper of the second floor. Paul D could see just the beginning of the paper; discreet flecks of yellow sprinkled among a blizzard of snowdrops all backed by blue. The luminous white of the railing and steps kept him glancing toward it. Every sense he had told him the air above the stairwell was charmed and very thin. But the girl who walked down out of that air was round and brown with the face of an alert doll.

Paul D looked at the girl and then at Sethe who smiled saying, 'Here she is my Denver. This is Paul D, honey, from Sweet Home.'

'Good morning, Mr D.'

'Garner, baby. Paul D Garner.'

'Yes sir.'

'Glad to get a look at you. Last time I saw your mama, you were pushing out the front of her dress.'

'Still is,' Sethe smiled, 'provided she can get in it.'

Denver stood on the bottom step and was suddenly hot and shy. It had been a long time since anybody (good-willed whitewoman, preacher, speaker or newspaperman) sat at their table, their sympathetic voices called liar by the revulsion in their eyes. For twelve years, long before Grandma Baby died, there had been no visitors of any sort and certainly no friends. No coloredpeople. Certainly no hazelnut man with too long hair and no notebook, no charcoal, no oranges, no questions. Someone her mother wanted to talk to and would even consider talking to while barefoot. Looking, in fact acting, like a girl instead of the quiet, queenly woman Denver had known all her life. The one who never looked away, who when a man got stomped to death by a mare right in front of Sawyer's restaurant did not look away; and when a sow began eating her own litter did not look away then either. And when the baby's spirit picked up Here Boy and slammed him into the wall hard enough to break two of his legs and dislocate his eye, so hard he went into convulsions and chewed up his tongue, still her mother had not looked away. She had taken a hammer, knocked the dog unconscious, wiped away the blood and saliva, pushed his eye back in his head and set his leg bones. He recovered, mute and off-balance, more because of his untrustworthy eye than his bent legs, and winter, summer, drizzle or dry, nothing could persuade him to enter the house again.

Now here was this woman with the presence of mind to repair a dog gone savage with pain rocking her crossed ankles and looking away from her own daughter's body. As though the size of it was more than vision could bear. And neither she nor he had on shoes. Hot, shy, now Denver was lonely. All that leaving: first her brothers, then her grandmother – serious losses since there were no children willing to circle her in a game or hang by their knees from her porch railing. None of that had mattered as long as her mother did not look away as she was doing now, making Denver long, downright *long*, for a sign of spite from the baby ghost.

'She's a fine-looking young lady,' said Paul D. 'Fine-looking. Got her daddy's sweet face.'

'You know my father?'

'Knew him. Knew him well.'

'Did he, Ma'am?' Denver fought an urge to realign her affection.

'Of course he knew your daddy. I told you, he's from Sweet Home.'

Denver sat down on the bottom step. There was nowhere else gracefully to go. They were a twosome, saying 'Your daddy' and 'Sweet Home' in a way that made it clear both belonged to them and not to her. That her own father's absence was not hers. Once the absence had belonged to Grandma Baby – a son, deeply mourned because he was the one who had bought her out of there. Then it was her mother's absent husband. Now it was this hazelnut stranger's absent friend. Only those who knew him ('knew him well') could claim his absence for themselves. Just as only those who lived in Sweet Home could remember it, whisper it and glance sideways at one another while they did. Again she wished for the baby ghost – its anger thrilling her now where it used to wear her out. Wear her out.

'We have a ghost in here,' she said, and it worked. They were not a twosome anymore. Her mother left off swinging her feet and being girlish. Memory of Sweet Home dropped away from the eyes of the man she was being girlish for. He looked quickly up the lightning-white stairs behind her.

'So I hear,' he said. 'But sad, your mama said. Not evil.'

'No sir,' said Denver, 'not evil. But not sad either.'

'What then?'

'Rebuked. Lonely and rebuked.'

'Is that right?' Paul D turned to Sethe.

'I don't know about lonely,' said Denver's mother. 'Mad, maybe, but I don't see how it could be lonely spending every minute with us like it does.'

'Must be something you got it wants.'

Sethe shrugged. 'It's just a baby.'

'My sister,' said Denver. 'She died in this house.'

Paul D scratched the hair under his jaw. 'Reminds me of that headless bride back behind Sweet Home. Remember that, Sethe? Used to roam them woods regular.'

'How could I forget? Worrisome . . .'

'How come everybody run off from Sweet Home can't stop talking about it? Look like if it was so sweet you would have stayed.'

'Girl, who you talking to?'

Paul D laughed. 'True, true. She's right, Sethe. It wasn't sweet and it sure wasn't home.' He shook his head.

'But it's where we were,' said Sethe. 'All together. Comes back whether we want it to or not.' She shivered a little. A light ripple of skin on her arm, which she caressed back into sleep. 'Denver,' she said, 'start up that stove. Can't have a friend stop by and don't feed him.'

'Don't go to any trouble on my account,' Paul D said.

'Bread ain't trouble. The rest I brought back from where I work. Least I can do, cooking from dawn to noon, is bring dinner home. You got any objections to pike?'

'If he don't object to me I don't object to him.'

At it again, thought Denver. Her back to them, she jostled the kindlin and almost lost the fire. 'Why don't you spend the night, Mr Garner? You and Ma'am can talk about Sweet Home all night long.'

Sethe took two swift steps to the stove, but before she could yank Denver's collar, the girl leaned forward and began to cry.

'What is the matter with you? I never knew you to behave this way.'

'Leave her be,' said Paul D. 'I'm a stranger to her.'

'That's just it. She got no cause to act up with a stranger. Oh baby, what is it? Did something happen?'

But Denver was shaking now and sobbing so she could not speak. The tears she had not shed for nine years wetting her far too womanly breasts.

'I can't no more. I can't no more.'

'Can't what? What can't you?'

'I can't live here. I don't know where to go or what to do, but I can't live here. Nobody speaks to us. Nobody comes by. Boys don't like me. Girls don't either.'

'Honey, honey.'

'What's she talking 'bout nobody speaks to you?' asked Paul D.

'It's the house. People don't –'

'It's not! It's not the house. It's us! And it's you!'

'Denver!'

'Leave off, Sethe. It's hard for a young girl living in a haunted house. That can't be easy.'

'It's easier than some other things.'

'Think, Sethe. I'm a grown man with nothing new left to see or do and I'm telling you it ain't easy. Maybe you all ought to move. Who owns this house?'

Over Denver's shoulder Sethe shot Paul D a look of snow. 'What you care?'

'They won't let you leave?'

'No.'

'Sethe.'

'No moving. No leaving. It's all right the way it is.'

'You going to tell me it's all right with this child half out of her mind?'

Something in the house braced, and in the listening quiet that followed Sethe spoke.

'I got a tree on my back and a haint in my house, and nothing in between but the daughter I am holding in my arms. No more running – from nothing. I will never run from another thing on this earth. I took one journey and I paid for the ticket, but let me tell you something, Paul D Garner: it cost too much! Do you hear me? It cost too much. Now sit down and eat with us or leave us be.'

Paul D fished in his vest for a little pouch of tobacco – concentrating on its contents and the knot of its string while Sethe led Denver into the keeping room that opened off the large room he was sitting in. He had no smoking papers, so he fiddled with the pouch and listened through the open door to Sethe quieting her daughter. When she came back she avoided his look and went straight to a

No more running –
from nothing. I will
never run from another
thing on this earth

small table next to the stove. Her back was to him and he could see all the hair he wanted without the distraction of her face.

'What tree on your back?'

'Huh.' Sethe put a bowl on the table and reached under it for flour.

'What tree on your back? Is something growing on your back? I don't see nothing growing on your back.'

'It's there all the same.'

'Who told you that?'

'Whitegirl. That's what she called it. I've never seen it and never will. But that's what she said it looked like. A chokecherry tree. Trunk, branches, and even leaves. Tiny little chokecherry leaves. But that was eighteen years ago. Could have cherries too now for all I know.'

Sethe took a little spit from the tip of her tongue with her forefinger. Quickly, lightly she touched the stove. Then she trailed her fingers through the flour, parting, separating small hills and ridges of it, looking for mites. Finding none, she poured soda and salt into the crease of her folded hand and tossed both into the flour. Then she reached into a can and scooped half a handful of lard. Deftly she squeezed the flour through it, then with her left hand sprinkling water, she formed the dough.

'I had milk,' she said. 'I was pregnant with Denver but I had milk for my baby girl. I hadn't stopped nursing her when I sent her on ahead with Howard and Buglar.'

Now she rolled the dough out with a wooden pin.

'Anybody could smell me long before he saw me. And when he saw me he'd see the drops of it on the front of my dress. Nothing I could do about that. All I knew was I had to get my milk to my baby girl. Nobody was going to nurse her like me. Nobody was going to get it to her fast enough, or take it away when she had enough and didn't know it. Nobody knew that she couldn't pass her air if you held her up on your shoulder, only if she was lying on my knees. Nobody knew that but me and nobody had her milk but me. I told that to the women in the wagon. Told them to put sugar water in cloth to suck from so when I got there in a few days she wouldn't have forgot me. The milk would be there and I would be there with it.'

'Men don't know nothing much,' said Paul D, tucking his pouch back into his vest pocket, 'but they do know a suckling can't be away from its mother for long.'

'Then they know what it's like to send your children off when your breasts are full.'

'We was talking 'bout a tree, Sethe.'

'After I left you, those boys came in there and took my milk. That's what they came in there for. Held me down and took it. I told Mrs Garner on em. She had that lump and couldn't speak but her eyes rolled out tears. Them boys found out I told on em. Schoolteacher made one open up my back, and when it closed it made a tree. It grows there still.'

'They used cowhide on you?'

'And they took my milk.'

'They beat you and you was pregnant?'

'And they took my milk!'

The fat white circles of dough lined the pan in rows. Once more Sethe touched a wet forefinger to the stove. She opened the oven door and slid the pan of biscuits in. As she raised up from the heat she felt Paul D behind her and his hands under her breasts. She straightened up and knew, but could not feel, that his cheek was pressing into the branches of her chokecherry tree.

Not even trying, he had become the kind of man who could walk into a house and make the women cry. Because with him, in his presence, they could. There was something blessed in his manner. Women saw him and wanted to weep – to tell him that their chest hurt and their knees did too. Strong women and wise saw him and told him things they only told each other: that way past the Change of Life, desire in them had suddenly become enormous, greedy, more savage than when they were fifteen, and that it embarrassed them and made them sad; that secretly they longed to die – to be quit of it – that sleep was more precious to them than any waking day. Young girls sidled up to him to confess or describe how well-dressed the visitations were that had followed them straight from their dreams. Therefore, although he did not understand why this was so, he was not surprised when Denver dripped tears into the stovefire. Nor, fifteen minutes later, after telling him about her stolen milk, her mother wept as well. Behind her, bending down, his body an arc of kindness, he held her breasts in the palms of his hands. He rubbed his cheek on her back and learned that way her sorrow, the roots of it; its wide trunk and intricate branches. Raising his fingers to the hooks of her dress, he knew without seeing them or hearing any sigh that the tears were coming fast. And when the top of her dress was around her hips and he saw the sculpture her back had become, like the decorative work of an ironsmith too passionate for display, he could think but not say, 'Aw, Lord, girl.' And he would tolerate no peace until he had touched every ridge and leaf of it with his mouth, none of which Sethe could feel because her back skin had been dead for years. What she knew was that the responsibility for her breasts, at last, was in somebody else's hands.

Would there be a little space, she wondered, a little time, some way to hold off eventfulness, to push busyness into the corners of the room and just stand there a minute or two, naked from shoulder blade to waist, relieved of the weight of her breasts, smelling the stolen milk again and the pleasure of baking bread? Maybe this one time she could stop dead still in the middle of a cooking meal – not even leave the stove – and feel the hurt her back ought to. Trust things and remember things because the last of the Sweet Home men was there to catch her if she sank?

WHEN DENVER LOOKED in, she saw her mother on her knees in prayer, which was not unusual. What was unusual (even for a girl who had lived all her life in a house peopled

by the living activity of the dead) was that a white dress
knelt down next to her mother and had its sleeve around
her mother's waist. And it was the tender embrace of the
dress sleeve that made Denver remember the details of
her birth – that and the thin, whipping snow she was
standing in, like the fruit of common flowers. The dress
and her mother together looked like two friendly
grown-up women – one (the dress) helping out the other.
And the magic of her birth, its miracle in fact, testified to
that friendliness as did her own name.

   Easily she stepped into the told story that lay before
her eyes on the path she followed away from the window.
There was only one door to the house and to get to it from
the back you had to walk all the way around to the front
of 124, past the storeroom, past the cold house, the privy,
the shed, on around to the porch. And to get to the part
of the story she liked best, she had to start way back:
hear the birds in the thick woods, the crunch of leaves
underfoot; see her mother making her way up into the
hills where no houses were likely to be. How Sethe was
walking on two feet meant for standing still. How they
were so swollen she could not see her arch or feel her
ankles. Her leg shaft ended in a loaf of flesh scalloped by
five toenails. But she could not, would not, stop, for when
she did the little antelope rammed her with horns and
pawed the ground of her womb with impatient hooves.
While she was walking, it seemed to graze, quietly – so
she walked, on two feet meant, in this sixth month of

pregnancy, for standing still. Still, near a kettle; still, at the churn; still, at the tub and ironing board. Milk, sticky and sour on her dress, attracted every small flying thing from gnats to grasshoppers. By the time she reached the hill skirt she had long ago stopped waving them off. The clanging in her head, begun as a churchbell heard from a distance, was by then a tight cap of pealing bells around her ears. She sank and had to look down to see whether she was in a hole or kneeling. Nothing was alive but her nipples and the little antelope. Finally, she was horizontal – or must have been because blades of wild onion were scratching her temple and her cheek. Concerned as she was for the life of her children's mother, Sethe told Denver, she remembered thinking: Well, at least I don't have to take another step. A dying thought if ever there was one, and she waited for the little antelope to protest, and why she thought of an antelope Sethe could not imagine since she had never seen one. She guessed it must have been an invention held on to from before Sweet Home, when she was very young. Of that place where she was born (Carolina maybe? or was it Louisiana?) she remembered only song and dance. Not even her own mother, who was pointed out to her by the eight-year-old child who watched over the young ones – pointed out as the one among many backs turned away from her, stooping in a watery field. Patiently Sethe waited for this particular back to gain the row's end and stand. What she saw was a cloth hat as opposed to a straw one, singularity enough in that world of cooing women each of whom was called Ma'am.

'Seth–thuh.'

'Ma'am.'

'Hold on to the baby.'

'Yes, Ma'am.'

'Seth–thuh.'

'Ma'am.'

'Get some kindlin in here.'

'Yes, Ma'am.'

Oh but when they sang. And oh but when they danced and sometimes they danced the antelope. The men as well as the ma'ams, one of whom was certainly her own. They shifted shapes and became something other. Some unchained, demanding other whose feet knew her pulse better than she did. Just like this one in her stomach.

'I believe this baby's ma'am is gonna die in wild onions on the bloody side of the Ohio River.' That's what was on her mind and what she told Denver. Her exact words. And it didn't seem such a bad idea, all in all, in view of the step she would not have to take, but the thought of herself stretched out dead while the little antelope lived on – an hour? a day? a day and a night? – in her lifeless body grieved her so she made the groan that made the person walking on a path not ten yards away halt and stand right still. Sethe had not heard the walking, but suddenly she heard the standing still and then she smelled the hair. The voice, saying, 'Who's in there?' was all she needed to know that she was about to be discovered by a whiteboy. That he too had mossy teeth, an appetite. That on a ridge of pine near the Ohio River, trying to get to her three children, one of whom was starving for the food she carried; that after her husband had disappeared; that after her milk had been stolen, her back pulped, her children orphaned, she was not to have an easeful death. No.

She told Denver that a *something* came up out of the earth into her – like a freezing, but moving too, like jaws inside. 'Look like I was just cold jaws grinding,' she said. Suddenly she was eager for his eyes, to bite into them; to gnaw his cheek.

'I was hungry,' she told Denver, 'just as hungry as I could be for his eyes. I couldn't wait.'

So she raised up on her elbow and dragged herself, one pull, two, three, four, toward the young white voice talking about 'Who that back in there?'

'"Come see," I was thinking. "Be the last thing you behold," and sure enough here come the feet so I thought well that's where I'll have to start God do what He would, I'm gonna eat his feet off. I'm laughing now, but it's true. I wasn't just set to do it. I was hungry to do it. Like a snake. All jaws and hungry.

'It wasn't no whiteboy at all. Was a girl. The raggediest-looking trash you ever saw saying, "Look there. A nigger. If that don't beat all."'

And now the part Denver loved the best:

Her name was Amy and she needed beef and pot liquor

like nobody in this world. Arms like cane stalks and enough hair for four or five heads. Slow-moving eyes. She didn't look at anything quick. Talked so much it wasn't clear how she could breathe at the same time. And those cane-stalk arms, as it turned out, were as strong as iron.

'You 'bout the scariest-looking something I ever seen. What you doing back up in here?'

Down in the grass, like the snake she believed she was, Sethe opened her mouth, and instead of fangs and a split tongue, out shot the truth.

'Running,' Sethe told her. It was the first word she had spoken all day and it came out thick because of her tender tongue.

'Them the feet you running on? My Jesus my.' She squatted down and stared at Sethe's feet. 'You got anything on you, gal, pass for food?'

'No.' Sethe tried to shift to a sitting position but couldn't.

'I like to die I'm so hungry.' The girl moved her eyes slowly, examining the greenery around her. 'Thought there'd be huckleberries. Look like it. That's why I come up in here. Didn't expect to find no nigger woman. If they was any, birds ate em. You like huckleberries?'

'I'm having a baby, miss.'

Amy looked at her. 'That mean you don't have no appetite? Well I got to eat me something.'

Combing her hair with her fingers, she carefully surveyed the landscape once more. Satisfied nothing edible was around, she stood up to go and Sethe's heart stood up too at the thought of being left alone in the grass without a fang in her head.

'Where you on your way to, miss?'

She turned and looked at Sethe with freshly lit eyes. 'Boston. Get me some velvet. It's a store there called Wilson. I seen the pictures of it and they have the prettiest velvet. They don't believe I'm a get it, but I am.'

Sethe nodded and shifted her elbow. 'Your ma'am know you on the lookout for velvet?'

The girl shook her hair out of her face. 'My mama worked for these here people to pay for her passage. But then she had me and since she died right after, well, they said I had to work for em to pay it off. I did, but now I want me some velvet.'

They did not look directly at each other, not straight into the eyes anyway. Yet they slipped effortlessly into yard chat about nothing in particular – except one lay on the ground.

'Boston,' said Sethe. 'Is that far?'

'Ooooh, yeah. A hundred miles. Maybe more.'

'Must be velvet closer by.'

'Not like in Boston. Boston got the best. Be so pretty on me. You ever touch it?'

'No, miss. I never touched no velvet.' Sethe didn't know if it was the voice, or Boston or velvet, but while the white-girl talked, the baby slept. Not one butt or kick, so she guessed her luck had turned.

'Ever see any?' she asked Sethe. 'I bet you never even seen any.'

'If I did I didn't know it. What's it like, velvet?'

Amy dragged her eyes over Sethe's face as though she would never give out so confidential a piece of information as that to a perfect stranger.

'What they call you?' she asked.

However far she was from Sweet Home, there was no point in giving out her real name to the first person she saw. 'Lu,' said Sethe. 'They call me Lu.'

'Well, Lu, velvet is like the world was just born. Clean and new and so smooth. The velvet I seen was brown, but in Boston they got all colors. Carmine. That means red but when you talk about velvet you got to say "carmine."' She raised her eyes to the sky and then, as though she had wasted enough time away from Boston, she moved off saying, 'I gotta go.'

Picking her way through the brush she hollered back to Sethe, 'What you gonna do, just lay there and foal?'

'I can't get up from here,' said Sethe.

'What?' She stopped and turned to hear.

'I said I can't get up.'

Amy drew her arm across her nose and came slowly back to where Sethe lay. 'It's a house back yonder,' she said.

'A house?'

'Mmmmm. I passed it. Ain't no regular house with people in it though. A lean-to, kinda.'

'How far?'

'Make a difference, does it? You stay the night here snake get you.'

'Well he may as well come on. I can't stand up let alone walk and God help me, miss, I can't crawl.'

'Sure you can, Lu. Come on,' said Amy and, with a toss of hair enough for five heads, she moved toward the path.

So she crawled and Amy walked alongside her, and when Sethe needed to rest, Amy stopped too and talked some more about Boston and velvet and good things to eat. The sound of that voice, like a sixteen-year-old boy's, going on and on and on, kept the little antelope quiet and grazing. During the whole hateful crawl to the lean-to, it never bucked once.

Nothing of Sethe's was intact by the time they reached it except the cloth that covered her hair. Below her bloody knees, there was no feeling at all; her chest was two cushions of pins. It was the voice full of velvet and Boston and good things to eat that urged her along and made her think that maybe she wasn't, after all, just a crawling graveyard for a six-month baby's last hours.

The lean-to was full of leaves, which Amy pushed into a pile for Sethe to lie on. Then she gathered rocks, covered them with more leaves and made Sethe put her feet on them, saying: 'I know a woman had her feet cut off they was so swole.' And she made sawing gestures with the blade of her hand across Sethe's ankles. 'Zzz Zzz Zzz Zzz.'

'I used to be a good size. Nice arms and everything. Wouldn't think it, would you? That was before they put me in the root cellar. I was fishing off the Beaver once. Catfish in Beaver River sweet as chicken. Well I was just fishing there and a nigger floated right by me. I don't like drowned people, you? Your feet remind me of him. All swole like.'

Then she did the magic: lifted Sethe's feet and legs and massaged them until she cried salt tears.

'It's gonna hurt, now,' said Amy. 'Anything dead coming back to life hurts.'

'Recitatif', a short story

MY MOTHER DANCED all night and Roberta's was sick. That's why we were taken to St Bonny's. People want to put their arms around you when you tell them you were in a shelter, but it really wasn't bad. No big long room with one hundred beds like Bellevue. There were four to a room, and when Roberta and me came, there was a shortage of state kids, so we were the only ones assigned to 406 and could go from bed to bed if we wanted to. And we wanted to, too. We changed beds every night and for the whole four months we were there we never picked one out as our own permanent bed.

It didn't start out that way. The minute I walked in and the Big Bozo introduced us, I got sick to my stomach. It was one thing to be taken out of your own bed early in the morning – it was something else to be stuck in a strange place with a girl from a whole other race. And Mary, that's my mother, she was right. Every now and then she would stop dancing long enough to tell me something important and one of the things she said was that they never washed their hair and they smelled funny. Roberta sure did. Smell funny, I mean. So when the Big Bozo (nobody ever called her Mrs Itkin, just like nobody every said St Bonaventure) – when she said, 'Twyla, this is Roberta. Roberta, this is Twyla. Make each other welcome,' I said, 'My mother won't like you putting me in here.'

'Good,' said Bozo. 'Maybe then she'll come and take you home.'

How's that for mean? If Roberta had laughed I would have killed her, but she didn't. She just walked over to the window and stood with her back to us.

'Turn around,' said the Bozo. 'Don't be rude. Now Twyla. Roberta. When you hear a loud buzzer, that's the call for dinner. Come down to the first floor. Any fights and no movie.' And then, just to make sure we knew what we would be missing, 'The Wizard of Oz.'

Roberta must have thought I meant that my mother would be mad about my being put in the shelter. Not about rooming with her, because as soon as Bozo left she came over to me and said, 'Is your mother sick too?'

'No,' I said. 'She just likes to dance all night.'

'Oh,' she nodded her head and I liked the way she understood things so fast. So for the moment it didn't matter that we looked like salt and pepper standing there and that's what the other kids called us sometimes. We were eight years old and got F's all the time. Me because I couldn't remember what I read or what the teacher said.

And Roberta because she couldn't read at all and didn't even listen to the teacher. She wasn't good at anything except jacks, at which she was a killer: pow scoop pow scoop pow scoop.

We didn't like each other all that much at first, but nobody else wanted to play with us because we weren't real orphans with beautiful dead parents in the sky. We were dumped. Even the New York City Puerto Ricans and the upstate Indians ignored us. All kinds of kids were in there, black ones, white ones, even two Koreans. The food was good, though. At least I thought so. Roberta hated it and left whole pieces of things on her plate: Spam, Salisbury steak – even jello with fruit cocktail in it, and she didn't care if I ate what she wouldn't. Mary's idea of supper was popcorn and a can of Yoo-Hoo. Hot mashed potatoes and two weenies was like Thanksgiving for me.

It really wasn't bad, St Bonny's. The big girls on the second floor pushed us around now and then. But that was all. They wore lipstick and eyebrow pencil and wobbled their knees while they watched TV. Fifteen, sixteen, even, some of them were. They were put-out girls, scared runaways most of them. Poor little girls who fought their uncles off but looked tough to us, and mean. God did they look mean. The staff tried to keep them separate from the younger children, but sometimes they caught us watching them in the orchard where they played radios and danced with each other. They'd light out after us and pull our hair or twist our arms. We were scared of them, Roberta and me, but neither of us wanted the other one to know it. So we got a good list of dirty names we could shout back when we ran from them through the orchard. I used to dream a lot and almost always the orchard was there. Two acres, four maybe, of these little apple trees. Hundreds of them. Empty and crooked like beggar women when I first came to St Bonny's but fat with flowers when I left. I don't know why I dreamt about that orchard so much. Nothing really happened there. Nothing all that important, I mean. Just the big girls dancing and playing the radio. Roberta and me watching. Maggie fell down there once. The kitchen woman with legs like parentheses. And the big girls laughed at her. We should have helped her up, I know, but we were scared of those girls with lipstick and eyebrow pencil. Maggie couldn't talk. The kids said she had her tongue cut out, but I think she was just born that way: mute. She was old and sandy-colored and she worked in the kitchen. I don't know if she was nice or not. I just remember her legs like parentheses and how she rocked when she walked. She worked from early in the morning till two o'clock, and if she was late, if she had too much cleaning and didn't get out till two-fifteen or so, she'd cut through the orchard so she wouldn't miss her bus and have to wait another hour. She wore this really stupid little hat – a kid's hat with ear flaps – and she wasn't much taller than we were. A really awful little hat. Even for a mute, it was dumb – dressing like a kid and never saying anything at all.

'But what about if somebody tries to kill her?' I used to wonder about that. 'Or what if she wants to cry? Can she cry?'

'Sure,' Roberta said. 'But just tears. No sounds come out.'

'She can't scream?'

'Nope. Nothing.'

'Can she hear?'

'I guess.'

'Let's call her,' I said. And we did.

'Dummy! Dummy!' She never turned her head.

'Bow legs! Bow legs!' Nothing. She just rocked on, the chin straps of her baby-boy hat swaying from side to side. I think we were wrong. I think she could hear and didn't let on. And it shames me even now to think there was somebody in there after all who heard us call her those names and couldn't tell on us.

We got along all right, Roberta and me. Changed beds every night, got F's in civics and communication skills and gym. The Bozo was disappointed in us, she said. Out of 130 of us state cases, 90 were under twelve. Almost all were real orphans with beautiful dead parents in the sky. We were the only ones dumped and the only ones with F's in three classes including gym. So we got along – what with her leaving whole pieces of things on her plate and being nice about not asking questions.

I think it was the day before Maggie fell down that we found out our mothers were coming to visit us on the same Sunday. We had been at the shelter twenty-eight days (Roberta twenty-eight and a half) and this was their first visit with us. Our mothers would come at ten o'clock in time for chapel, then lunch with us in the teachers' lounge. I thought if my dancing mother met her sick mother it might be good for her. And Roberta thought her sick mother would get a big bang out of a dancing one. We got excited about it and curled each other's hair. After breakfast we sat on the bed watching the road from the window. Roberta's socks were still wet. She washed them the night before and put them on the radiator to dry. They hadn't, but she put them on anyway because their tops were so pretty – scalloped in pink. Each of us had a purple construction-paper basket that we had made in craft class. Mine had a yellow crayon rabbit on it. Roberta's had eggs with wiggly lines of color. Inside were cellophane grass and just the jelly beans because I'd eaten the two marshmallow eggs they gave us. The Big Bozo came herself to get us. Smiling she told us we looked very nice and to come downstairs. We were so surprised by the smile we'd never seen before, neither of us moved.

'Don't you want to see your mommies?'

I stood up first and spilled the jelly beans all over the floor. Bozo's smile disappeared while we scrambled to get the candy up off the floor and put it back in the grass.

She escorted us downstairs to the first floor, where the other girls were lining up to file into the chapel. A bunch of grown-ups stood to one side. Viewers mostly. The old

biddies who wanted servants and the fags who wanted
company looking for children they might want to adopt.
Once in a while a grandmother. Almost never anybody
young or anybody whose face wouldn't scare you in the
night. Because if any of the real orphans had young rela-
tives they wouldn't be real orphans. I saw Mary right
away. She had on those green slacks I hated and hated
even more now because didn't she know we were going to
chapel? And that fur jacket with the pocket linings so
ripped she had to pull to get her hands out of them. But
her face was pretty – like always, and she smiled and waved
like she was the little girl looking for her mother – not me.

I walked slowly, trying not to drop the jelly beans and
hoping the paper handle would hold. I had to use my last
Chiclet because by the time I finished cutting everything
out, all the Elmer's was gone. I am left-handed and the
scissors never worked for me. It didn't matter, though; I
might just as well have chewed the gum. Mary dropped to
her knees and grabbed me, mashing the basket, the jelly
beans, and the grass into her ratty fur jacket.

'Twyla, baby. Twyla, baby!'

I could have killed her. Already I heard the big girls in
the orchard the next time saying, 'Twyyyyyla, baby!' But
I couldn't stay mad at Mary while she was smiling and
hugging me and smelling of Lady Esther dusting powder.
I wanted to stay buried in her fur all day.

To tell the truth I forgot about Roberta. Mary and I got
in line for the traipse into chapel and I was feeling proud

because she looked so beautiful even in those ugly green slacks that made her behind stick out. A pretty mother on earth is better than a beautiful dead one in the sky even if she did leave you all alone to go dancing.

I felt a tap on my shoulder, turned, and saw Roberta smiling. I smiled back, but not too much lest somebody think this visit was the biggest thing that ever happened in my life. Then Roberta said, 'Mother, I want you to meet my roommate, Twyla. And that's Twyla's mother.'

I looked up it seemed for miles. She was big. Bigger than any man and on her chest was the biggest cross I'd ever seen. I swear it was six inches long each way. And in the crook of her arm was the biggest Bible ever made.

Mary, simple-minded as ever, grinned and tried to yank her hand out of the pocket with the raggedy lining – to shake hands, I guess. Roberta's mother looked down at me and then looked down at Mary too. She didn't say anything, just grabbed Roberta with her Bible-free hand and stepped out of line, walking quickly to the rear of it. Mary was still grinning because she's not too swift when it comes to what's really going on. Then this light bulb goes off in her head and she says 'That bitch!' really loud and us almost in the chapel now. Organ music whining; the Bonny Angels singing sweetly. Everybody in the world turned around to look. And Mary would have kept it up – kept calling names if I hadn't squeezed her hand as hard as I could. That helped a little, but she still twitched and crossed and uncrossed her legs all through service.

Even groaned a couple of times. Why did I think she would come there and act right? Slacks. No hat like the grandmothers and viewers, and groaning all the while. When we stood for hymns she kept her mouth shut. Wouldn't even look at the words on the page. She actually reached in her purse for a mirror to check her lipstick. All I could think of was that she really needed to be killed. The sermon lasted a year, and I knew the real orphans were looking smug again.

We were supposed to have lunch in the teachers' lounge, but Mary didn't bring anything, so we picked fur and cellophane grass off the mashed jelly beans and ate them. I could have killed her. I sneaked a look at Roberta. Her mother had brought chicken legs and ham sand-wiches and oranges and a whole box of chocolate-covered grahams. Roberta drank milk from a thermos while her mother read the Bible to her.

Things are not right. The wrong food is always with the wrong people. Maybe that's why I got into waitress work later – to match up the right people with the right food. Roberta just let those chicken legs sit there, but she did bring a stack of grahams up to me later when the visit was over. I think she was sorry that her mother would not shake my mother's hand. And I liked that and I liked the fact that she didn't say a word about Mary groaning all the way through the service and not bringing any lunch.

Roberta left in May when the apple trees were heavy and white. On her last day we went to the orchard to watch the big girls smoke and dance by the radio. It didn't matter that they said, 'Twyyyyyla, baby.' We sat on the ground and breathed. Lady Esther. Apple blossoms. I still go soft when I smell one or the other. Roberta was going home. The big cross and the big Bible was coming to get her and she seemed sort of glad and sort of not. I thought I would die in that room of four beds without her and I knew Bozo had plans to move some other dumped kid in there with me. Roberta promised to write every day, which was really sweet of her because she couldn't read a lick so how could she write anybody. I would have drawn pictures and sent them to her but she never gave me her address. Little by little she faded. Her wet socks with the pink scalloped tops and her big serious-looking eyes – that's all I could catch when I tried to bring her to mind.

I WAS WORKING behind the counter at the Howard Johnson's on the Thruway just before the Kingston exit. Not a bad job. Kind of a long ride from Newburgh, but okay once I got there. Mine was the second night shift – eleven to seven. Very light until a Greyhound checked in for breakfast around six-thirty. At that hour the sun was all the way clear of the hills behind the restaurant. The place looked better at night – more like shelter – but I loved it when the sun broke in, even if it did show all the cracks in the vinyl and the speckled floor looked dirty no matter what the mop boy did.

It was August and a bus crowd was just unloading.

They would stand around a long while: going to the john, and looking at gifts and junk-for-sale machines, reluctant to sit down so soon. Even to eat. I was trying to fill the coffee pots and get them all situated on the electric burners when I saw her. She was sitting in a booth smoking a cigarette with two guys smothered in head and facial hair. Her own hair was so big and wild I could hardly see her face. But the eyes. I would know them anywhere. She had on a powder-blue halter and shorts outfit and earrings the size of bracelets.

Talk about lipstick and eyebrow pencil. She made the big girls look like nuns. I couldn't get off the counter until seven o'clock, but I kept watching the booth in case they got up to leave before that. My replacement was on time for a change, so I counted and stacked my receipts as fast as I could and signed off. I walked over to the booths, smiling and wondering if she would remember me. Or even if she wanted to remember me. Maybe she didn't want to be reminded of St Bonny's or to have anybody know she was ever there. I know I never talked about it to anybody.

I put my hands in my apron pockets and leaned against the back of the booth facing them.

'Roberta? Roberta Fisk?'

She looked up. 'Yeah?'

'Twyla.'

She squinted for a second and then said, 'Wow.'

'Remember me?'

'Sure. Hey. Wow.'

'It's been a while,' I said, and gave a smile to the two hairy guys.

'Yeah. Wow. You work here?'

'Yeah,' I said. 'I live in Newburgh.'

'Newburgh? No kidding?' She laughed then, a private laugh that included the guys but only the guys, and they laughed with her. What could I do but laugh too and wonder why I was standing there with my knees showing out from under that uniform. Without looking I could see the blue and white triangle on my head, my hair shapeless in a net, my ankles thick in white oxfords. Nothing could have been less sheer than my stockings. There was this silence that came down right after I laughed. A silence it was her turn to fill up. With introductions, maybe, to her boyfriends or an invitation to sit down and have a Coke. Instead she lit a cigarette off the one she'd just finished and said, 'We're on our way to the Coast. He's got an appointment with Hendrix.'

She gestured casually toward the boy next to her.

'Hendrix? Fantastic,' I said. 'Really fantastic. What's she doing now?'

Roberta coughed on her cigarette and the two guys rolled their eyes up at the ceiling.

'Hendrix. Jimi Hendrix, asshole. He's only the biggest – Oh, wow. Forget it.'

I was dismissed without anyone saying goodbye, so I thought I would do it for her.

'How's your mother?' I asked. Her grin cracked her whole face. She swallowed. 'Fine,' she said. 'How's yours?'

'Pretty as a picture,' I said and turned away. The backs of my knees were damp. Howard Johnson's really was a dump in the sunlight.

JAMES IS AS comfortable as a house slipper. He liked my cooking and I liked his big loud family. They have lived in Newburgh all of their lives and talk about it the way people do who have always known a home. His grandmother is a porch swing older than his father and when they talk about streets and avenues and buildings they call them names they no longer have. They still call the A & P Rico's because it stands on property once a mom and pop store owned by Mr Rico. And they call the new community college Town Hall because it once was. My mother-in-law puts up jelly and cucumbers and buys butter wrapped in cloth from a dairy. James and his father talk about fishing and baseball and I can see them all together on the Hudson in a raggedy skiff. Half the population of Newburgh is on welfare now, but to my husband's family it was still some upstate paradise of a time long past. A time of ice houses and vegetable wagons, coal furnaces and children weeding gardens. When our son was born my mother-in-law gave me the crib blanket that had been hers.

But the town they remembered had changed. Something quick was in the air. Magnificent old houses, so ruined they had become shelter for squatters and rent risks, were bought and renovated. Smart IBM people moved out of their suburbs back into the city and put shutters up and herb gardens in their backyards. A brochure came in the mail announcing the opening of a Food Emporium. Gourmet food it said – and listed items the rich IBM crowd would want. It was located in a new mall at the edge of town and I drove out to shop there one day – just to see. It was late in June. After the tulips were gone and the Queen Elizabeth roses were open everywhere.

I trailed my cart along the aisle tossing in smoked oysters and Robert's sauce and things I knew would sit in my cupboard for years. Only when I found some Klondike ice cream bars did I feel less guilty about spending James's fireman's salary so foolishly. My father-in-law ate them with the same gusto little Joseph did.

Waiting in the check-out line I heard a voice say, 'Twyla!'

The classical music piped over the aisles had affected me and the woman leaning toward me was dressed to kill. Diamonds on her hand, a smart white summer dress. 'I'm Mrs Benson,' I said.

'Ho. Ho. The Big Bozo,' she sang.

For a split second I didn't know what she was talking about. She had a bunch of asparagus and two cartons of fancy water.

'Roberta!'

'Right.'

'For heaven's sake. Roberta.'

'You look great,' she said.

'So do you. Where are you? Herc? In Newburgh?'

'Yes. Over in Annandale.'

I was opening my mouth to say more when the cashier called my attention to her empty counter.

'Meet you outside.' Roberta pointed her finger and went into the express line.

I placed the groceries and kept myself from glancing around to check Roberta's progress. I remembered Howard Johnson's and looking for a chance to speak only to be greeted with a stingy 'wow.' But she was waiting for me and her huge hair was sleek now, smooth around a small, nicely shaped head. Shoes, dress, everything lovely and summery and rich. I was dying to know what happened to her, how she got from Jimi Hendrix to Annandale, a neighborhood full of doctors and IBM executives. Easy, I thought. Everything is so easy for them. They think they own the world.

'How long,' I asked her. 'How long have you been here?'

'A year. I got married to a man who lives here. And you, you're married too, right? Benson, you said.'

'Yeah. James Benson.'

'And is he nice?'

'Oh, is he nice?'

'Well, is he?' Roberta's eyes were steady as though she really meant the question and wanted an answer.

He's wonderful, Roberta. Wonderful.'

'So you're happy.'

'Very.'

'That's good,' she said and nodded her head. 'I always hoped you'd be happy. Any kids? I know you have kids.'

'One. A boy. How about you?'

'Four.'

'Four?'

She laughed. 'Step kids. He's a widower.'

'Oh.'

'Got a minute? Let's have a coffee.'

I thought about the Klondikes melting and the inconvenience of going all the way to my car and putting the bags in the trunk. Served me right for buying all that stuff I didn't need. Roberta was ahead of me.

'Put them in my car. It's right here.'

And then I saw the dark blue limousine.

'You married a Chinaman?'

'No,' she laughed. 'He's the driver.'

'Oh, my. If the Big Bozo could see you now.'

We both giggled. Really giggled. Suddenly, in just a pulse beat, twenty years disappeared and all of it came rushing back. The big girls (whom we called gar girls – Roberta's misheard word for the evil stone faces described in a civics class) there dancing in the orchard, the ploppy mashed potatoes, the double weenies, the Spam with pineapple. We went into the coffee shop holding onto one another and I tried to think why we were glad to see each other this time and not before. Once, twelve years ago, we passed like strangers. A black girl and a white girl meeting in a Howard Johnson's on the road and having nothing to say. One in a blue and white triangle waitress hat – the other on her way to see Hendrix. Now we were behaving like sisters separated for much too long. Those four short months were nothing in time. Maybe it was the thing itself. Just being there, together. Two little girls who knew what nobody else in the world knew – how not to ask questions. How to believe what had to be believed. There was politeness in that reluctance and generosity as well. Is your mother sick too? No, she dances all night. Oh – and an understanding nod.

We sat in a booth by the window and fell into recollection like veterans. 'Did you ever learn to read?'

'Watch.' She picked up the menu. 'Special of the day. Cream of corn soup. Entrees. Two dots and a wriggly line. Quiche. Chef salad, scallops . . .'

I was laughing and applauding when the waitress came up.

'Remember the Easter baskets?'

'And how we tried to introduce them?'

'Your mother with that cross like two telephone poles.'

'And yours with those tight slacks.'

We laughed so loudly heads turned and made the laughter harder to suppress.

'What happened to the Jimi Hendrix date?'

Roberta made a blow-out sound with her lips.

'When he died I thought about you.'

'Oh, you heard about him finally?'

'Finally. Come on, I was a small-town country waitress.'

'And I was a small-town country dropout. God, were we wild. I still don't know how I got out of there alive.'

'But you did.'

'I did. I really did. Now I'm Mrs Kenneth Norton.'

'Sounds like a mouthful.'

'It is.'

'Servants and all?'

Roberta held up two fingers.

'Ow! What does he do?'

'Computers and stuff. What do I know?'

'I don't remember a hell of a lot from those days, but Lord, St Bonny's is as clear as daylight. Remember Maggie? The day she fell down and those gar girls laughed at her?'

Roberta looked up from her salad and stared at me. 'Maggie didn't fall,' she said.

'Yes, she did. You remember.'

'No, Twyla. They knocked her down. Those girls pushed her down and tore her clothes. In the orchard.'

'I don't – that's not what happened.'

'Sure it is. In the orchard. Remember how scared we were?'

'Wait a minute. I don't remember any of that.'

'And Bozo was fired.'

'You're crazy. She was there when I left. You left before me.'

'I went back. You weren't there when they fired Bozo.'

'What?'

'Twice. Once for a year when I was about ten, another for two months when I was fourteen. That's when I ran away.'

'You ran away from St Bonny's?'

'I had to. What do you want? Me dancing in that orchard?'

'Are you sure about Maggie?'

'Of course I'm sure. You've blocked it, Twyla. It happened. Those girls had behavior problems, you know.'

'Didn't they, though. But why can't I remember the Maggie thing?'

'Believe me. It happened. And we were there.'

'Who did you room with when you went back?' I asked her as if I would know her. The Maggie thing was troubling me.

'Creeps. They tickled themselves in the night.'

My ears were itching and I wanted to go home suddenly. This was all very well but she couldn't just comb her hair, wash her face and pretend everything was hunky-dory. After the Howard Johnson's snub. And no apology. Nothing.

'Were you on dope or what that time at Howard Johnson's?' I tried to make my voice sound friendlier than I felt.

'Maybe, a little. I never did drugs much. Why?'

'I don't know; you acted sort of like you didn't want to know me then.'

'Oh, Twyla, you know how it was in those days: black-white. You know how everything was.'

But I didn't know. I thought it was just the opposite. Busloads of blacks and whites came into Howard Johnson's together. They roamed together then: students, musicians, lovers, protesters. You got to see everything at Howard Johnson's and blacks were very friendly with whites in those days.

But sitting there with nothing on my plate but two hard tomato wedges wondering about the melting Klondikes it seemed childish remembering the slight. We went to her car, and with the help of the driver, got my stuff into my station wagon.

'We'll keep in touch this time,' she said.

'Sure,' I said. 'Sure. Give me a call.'

'I will,' she said, and then just as I was sliding behind the wheel, she leaned into the window. 'By the way. Your mother. Did she ever stop dancing?'

I shook my head. 'No. Never.'

Roberta nodded.

'And yours? Did she ever get well?'

She smiled a tiny sad smile. 'No. She never did. Look, call me, okay?'

'Okay,' I said, but I knew I wouldn't. Roberta had messed up my past somehow with that business about Maggie. I wouldn't forget a thing like that. Would I?

STRIFE CAME TO us that fall. At least that's what the paper called it. Strife. Racial strife. The word made me

think of a bird – a big shrieking bird out of 1,000,000,000
B. C. Flapping its wings and cawing. Its eye with no lid
always bearing down on you. All day it screeched and at
night it slept on the rooftops. It woke you in the morning
and from the *Today* show to the eleven o'clock news it
kept you an awful company. I couldn't figure it out from
one day to the next. I knew I was supposed to feel something strong, but I didn't know what, and James wasn't
any help. Joseph was on the list of kids to be transferred
from the junior high school to another one at some
far-out-of-the-way place and I thought it was a good thing
until I heard it was a bad thing. I mean I didn't know. All
the schools seemed dumps to me, and the fact that one
was nicer looking didn't hold much weight. But the papers
were full of it and then the kids began to get jumpy. In
August, mind you. Schools weren't even open yet. I
thought Joseph might be frightened to go over there, but
he didn't seem scared so I forgot about it, until I found
myself driving along Hudson Street out there by the
school they were trying to integrate and saw a line of
women marching. And who do you suppose was in
line, big as life, holding a sign in front of her bigger than
her mother's cross? MOTHERS HAVE RIGHTS TOO!
it said.

I drove on, and then changed my mind. I circled the
block, slowed down, and honked my horn.

Roberta looked over and when she saw me she waved.
I didn't wave back, but I didn't move either. She handed

Racial strife. The word made me think of a bird – a big shrieking bird out of 1,000,000,000 B. C.

her sign to another woman and came over to where I was parked.

'Hi.'

'What are you doing?'

'Picketing. What's it look like?'

'What for?'

'What do you mean, "What for?" They want to take my kids and send them out of the neighborhood. They don't want to go.'

'So what if they go to another school? My boy's being bussed too, and I don't mind. Why should you?'

'It's not about us, Twyla. Me and you. It's about our kids.'

'What's more us than that?'

'Well, it is a free country.'

'Not yet, but it will be.'

'What the hell does that mean? I'm not doing anything to you.'

'You really think that?'

'I know it.'

'I wonder what made me think you were different.'

'I wonder what made me think you were different.'

'Look at them,' I said. 'Just look. Who do they think they are? Swarming all over the place like they own it. And now they think they can decide where my child goes to school. Look at them, Roberta. They're Bozos.'

Roberta turned around and looked at the women. Almost all of them were standing still now, waiting. Some were even edging toward us. Roberta looked at me out of some refrigerator behind her eyes. 'No, they're not. They're just mothers.'

'And what am I? Swiss cheese?'

'I used to curl your hair.'

'I hated your hands in my hair.'

The women were moving. Our faces looked mean to them of course and they looked as though they could not wait to throw themselves in front of a police car, or better yet, into my car and drag me away by my ankles. Now they surrounded my car and gently, gently began to rock it. I swayed back and forth like a sideways yo-yo. Automatically I reached for Roberta, like the old days in the orchard when they saw us watching them and we had to get out of there, and if one of us fell the other pulled her up and if one of us was caught the other stayed to kick and scratch, and neither would leave the other behind. My arm shot out of the car window but no receiving hand was there. Roberta was looking at me sway from side to side in the car and her face was still. My purse slid from the car seat down under the dashboard. The four policemen who had been drinking Tab in their car finally got the message and strolled over, forcing their way through the women. Quietly, firmly they spoke. 'Okay, ladies. Back in line or off the streets.'

Some of them went away willingly; others had to be urged away from the car doors and the hood. Roberta didn't move. She was looking steadily at me. I was fumbling to turn on the ignition, which wouldn't catch because the gearshift was still in drive. The seats of the car were a mess because the swaying had thrown my grocery coupons all over it and my purse was sprawled on the floor.

'Maybe I am different now, Twyla. But you're not. You're the same little state kid who kicked a poor old black lady when she was down on the ground. You kicked a black lady and you have the nerve to call me a bigot.'

The coupons were everywhere and the guts of my purse were bunched under the dashboard. What was she saying? Black? Maggie wasn't black.

'She wasn't black,' I said.

'Like hell she wasn't, and you kicked her. We both did. You kicked a black lady who couldn't even scream.'

'Liar!'

'You're the liar! Why don't you just go on home and leave us alone, huh?'

She turned away and I skidded away from the curb.

The next morning I went into the garage and cut the side out of the carton our portable TV had come in. It wasn't nearly big enough, but after a while I had a decent sign: red spray-painted letters on a white background – AND SO DO CHILDREN****. I meant just to go down to the school and tack it up somewhere so those cows on the picket line across the street could see it, but when I got there, some ten or so others had already assembled – protesting the cows across the street. Police permits and everything. I got in line and we strutted in time on our side while Roberta's group strutted on theirs. That first day we were all dignified, pretending the other side didn't exist. The second day there was name calling and finger gestures. But that was about all. People changed signs from time to time, but Roberta never did and neither did I. Actually my sign didn't make sense without Roberta's. 'And so do children what?' one of the women on my side asked me. Have rights, I said, as though it was obvious.

Roberta didn't acknowledge my presence in any way and I got to thinking maybe she didn't know I was there. I began to pace myself in the line, jostling people one minute and lagging behind the next, so Roberta and I could reach the end of our respective lines at the same time and there would be a moment in our turn when we would face each other. Still, I couldn't tell whether she saw me and knew my sign was for her. The next day I went early before we were scheduled to assemble. I waited until she got there before I exposed my new creation. As soon as she hoisted her MOTHERS HAVE RIGHTS TOO I began to wave my new one, which said, HOW WOULD YOU KNOW? I know she saw that one, but I had gotten addicted now. My signs got crazier each day, and the women on my side decided that I was a kook. They couldn't make heads or tails out of my brilliant screaming posters.

I brought a painted sign in queenly red with huge black

letters that said, IS YOUR MOTHER WELL? Roberta took her lunch break and didn't come back for the rest of the day or any day after. Two days later I stopped going too and couldn't have been missed because nobody understood my signs anyway.

It was a nasty six weeks. Classes were suspended and Joseph didn't go to anybody's school until October. The children – everybody's children – soon got bored with that extended vacation they thought was going to be so great. They looked at TV until their eyes flattened. I spent a couple of mornings tutoring my son, as the other mothers said we should. Twice I opened a text from last year that he had never turned in. Twice he yawned in my face. Other mothers organized living room sessions so the kids would keep up. None of the kids could concentrate so they drifted back to *The Price Is Right* and *The Brady Bunch*. When the school finally opened there were fights once or twice and some sirens roared through the streets every once in a while. There were a lot of photographers from Albany. And just when ABC was about to send up a news crew, the kids settled down like nothing in the world had happened. Joseph hung my HOW WOULD YOU KNOW? sign in his bedroom. I don't know what became of AND SO DO CHILDREN****. I think my father-in-law cleaned some fish on it. He was always puttering around in our garage. Each of his five children lived in Newburgh and he acted as though he had five extra homes.

I couldn't help looking for Roberta when Joseph graduated from high school, but I didn't see her. It didn't trouble me much what she had said to me in the car. I mean the kicking part. I know I didn't do that, I couldn't do that. But I was puzzled by her telling me Maggie was black. When I thought about it I actually couldn't be certain. She wasn't pitch-black, I knew, or I would have remembered that. What I remember was the kiddie hat, and the semi-circle legs. I tried to reassure myself about the race thing for a long time until it dawned on me that the truth was already there, and Roberta knew it. I didn't kick her; I didn't join in with the gar girls and kick that lady, but I sure did want to. We watched and never tried to help her and never called for help. Maggie was my dancing mother. Deaf, I thought, and dumb. Nobody inside. Nobody who would hear you if you cried in the night. Nobody who could tell you anything important that you could use. Rocking, dancing, swaying as she walked. And when the gar girls pushed her down, and started roughhousing, I knew she wouldn't scream, couldn't – just like me and I was glad about that.

WE DECIDED NOT to have a tree, because Christmas would be at my mother-in-law's house, so why have a tree at both places? Joseph was at SUNY New Paltz and we had to economize, we said. But at the last minute, I changed my mind. Nothing could be that bad. So I rushed around town looking for a tree, something small but wide.

By the time I found a place, it was snowing and very late. I dawdled like it was the most important purchase in the world and the tree man was fed up with me. Finally I chose one and had it tied onto the trunk of the car. I drove away slowly because the sand trucks were not out yet and the streets could be murder at the beginning of a snow-fall. Downtown the streets were wide and rather empty except for a cluster of people coming out of the Newburgh Hotel. The one hotel in town that wasn't built out of card-board and Plexiglas. A party, probably. The men huddled in the snow were dressed in tails and the women had on furs. Shiny things glittered from underneath their coats. It made me tired to look at them. Tired, tired, tired. On the next corner was a small diner with loops and loops of paper bells in the window. I stopped the car and went in. Just for a cup of coffee and twenty minutes of peace before I went home and tried to finish everything before Christmas Eve.

'Twyla?'

There she was. In a silvery evening gown and dark fur coat. A man and another woman were with her, the man fumbling for change to put in the cigarette machine. The woman was humming and tapping on the counter with her fingernails. They all looked a little bit drunk.

'Well. It's you.'

'How are you?'

I shrugged. 'Pretty good. Frazzled. Christmas and all.'

'Regular?' called the woman from the counter.

'Fine,' Roberta called back and then, 'Wait for me in the car.'

She slipped into the booth beside me. 'I have to tell you something, Twyla. I made up my mind if I ever saw you again, I'd tell you.'

'I'd just as soon not hear anything, Roberta. It doesn't matter now, anyway.'

'No,' she said. 'Not about that.'

'Don't be long,' said the woman. She carried two regulars to go and the man peeled his cigarette pack as they left.

'It's about St Bonny's and Maggie.'

'Oh, please.'

'Listen to me. I really did think she was black. I didn't make that up. I really thought so. But now I can't be sure. I just remember her as old, so old. And because she couldn't talk – well, you know, I thought she was crazy. She'd been brought up in an institution like my mother was and like I thought I would be too. And you were right. We didn't kick her. It was the gar girls. Only them. But, well, I wanted to. I really wanted them to hurt her. I said we did it, too. You and me, but that's not true. And I don't want you to carry that around. It was just that I wanted to do it so bad that day – wanting to is doing it.'

Her eyes were watery from the drinks she'd had, I guess. I know it's that way with me. One glass of wine and I start bawling over the littlest thing.

'We were kids, Roberta.'

'Yeah. Yeah. I know, just kids.'

'Eight.'

'Eight.'

'And lonely.'

'Scared, too.'

She wiped her cheeks with the heel of her hand and smiled. 'Well that's all I wanted to say.'

I nodded and couldn't think of any way to fill the silence that went from the diner past the paper bells on out into the snow. It was heavy now. I thought I'd better wait for the sand trucks before starting home.

'Thanks, Roberta.'

'Sure.'

'Did I tell you? My mother, she never did stop dancing.'

'Yes. You told me. And mine, she never got well.' Roberta lifted her hands from the tabletop and covered her face with her palms. When she took them away she really was crying. 'Oh shit, Twyla. Shit, shit, shit. What the hell happened to Maggie?'

'Making America White Again', an essay

THIS IS A serious project. All immigrants to the United States know (and knew) that if they want to become real, authentic Americans they must reduce their fealty to their native country and regard it as secondary, subordinate, in order to emphasize their whiteness. Unlike any nation in Europe, the United States holds whiteness as the unifying force. Here, for many people, the definition of 'Americanness' is color.

Under slave laws, the necessity for color rankings was obvious, but in America today, post-civil-rights legislation, white people's conviction of their natural superiority is being lost. Rapidly lost. There are 'people of color' everywhere, threatening to erase this long-understood definition of America. And what then? Another black President? A predominantly black Senate? Three black Supreme Court Justices? The threat is frightening.

In order to limit the possibility of this untenable change, and restore whiteness to its former status as a marker of national identity, a number of white Americans are sacrificing themselves. They have begun *to do things they clearly don't really want to be doing*, and, to do so, they are (1) abandoning their sense of human dignity and (2) risking the appearance of cowardice. Much as they may hate their behavior, and know full well how craven it is, they are willing to kill small children attending Sunday school and slaughter churchgoers who invite a white boy to pray. Embarrassing as the obvious display of cowardice must be, they are willing to set fire to churches, and to start firing in them while the members are at prayer. And, shameful as such demonstrations of weakness are, they are willing to shoot black children in the street.

To keep alive the perception of white superiority, these white Americans tuck their heads under cone-shaped hats and American flags and deny themselves the dignity of face-to-face confrontation, training their guns on the unarmed, the innocent, the scared, on subjects who are running away, exposing their unthreatening backs to bullets. Surely, shooting a fleeing man in the back hurts the presumption of white strength? The sad plight of grown white men, crouching beneath their (better) selves, to slaughter the innocent during traffic stops, to push black women's faces into the dirt, to handcuff black children. Only the frightened would do that. Right?

These sacrifices, made by supposedly tough white men, who are prepared to abandon their humanity out of fear of black men and women, suggest the true horror of lost status.

It may be hard to feel pity for the men who are making these bizarre sacrifices in the name of white power and supremacy. Personal debasement is not easy for white people (especially for white men), but to retain the conviction of their superiority to others – especially to black people – they are willing to risk contempt, and to be reviled by the mature, the sophisticated, and the strong. If it weren't so ignorant and pitiful, one could mourn this collapse of dignity in service to an evil cause.

The comfort of being 'naturally better than,' of not having to struggle or demand civil treatment, is hard to give up. The confidence that you will not be watched in a department store, that you are the preferred customer in high-end restaurants – these social inflections, belonging to whiteness, are greedily relished.

So scary are the consequences of a collapse of white privilege that many Americans have flocked to a political platform that supports and translates violence against the defenseless as strength. These people are not so much angry as terrified, with the kind of terror that makes knees tremble.

On Election Day, how eagerly so many white voters – both the poorly educated and the well educated – embraced the shame and fear sowed by Donald Trump. The candidate whose company has been sued by the Justice Department for not renting apartments to black people.

The candidate who questioned whether Barack Obama was born in the United States, and who seemed to condone the beating of a Black Lives Matter protester at a campaign rally. The candidate who kept black workers off the floors of his casinos. The candidate who is beloved by David Duke and endorsed by the Ku Klux Klan.

William Faulkner understood this better than almost any other American writer. In 'Absalom, Absalom,' incest is less of a taboo for an upper-class Southern family than acknowledging the one drop of black blood that would clearly soil the family line. Rather than lose its 'whiteness' (once again), the family chooses murder.

© Toni Morrison

TONI MORRISON was born in Ohio in 1931. She began writing while teaching literature at Howard University and went on to publish her first novel, *The Bluest Eye* in 1970. She has since published eleven novels, including *Song of Solomon* and the Pulitzer-prize winning *Beloved*, as well as many non-fiction books and plays.

Morrison's writing is tirelessly engaged with issues of race and racism. *The Bluest Eye* explores what it means to be 'beautiful' in a world where whiteness monopolizes the mind, while *Beloved* plumbs the psychological pain and fracture, as well as the inconceivable sacrifices of those living under the tyranny of slavery. Her essay, 'Making America White Again' (which is also included in this book) examines the state of race relations in the Trump era.

Among the many prizes her work has been awarded, Morrison was presented with the Nobel Prize for Literature in 1993, and the Presidential Medal of Freedom in 2012.

RECOMMENDED BOOKS BY TONI MORRISON:

Beloved
Song of Solomon
The Bluest Eye

Hoping for some harmony after Race?

Sisters
LOUISA MAY ALCOTT

VINTAGE MINIS

Love
JEANETTE WINTERSON

VINTAGE MINIS

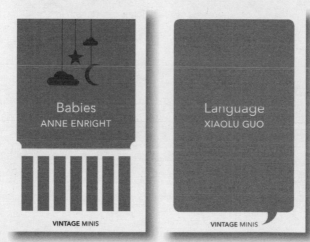

Babies
ANNE ENRIGHT

VINTAGE MINIS

Language
XIAOLU GUO

VINTAGE MINIS

VINTAGE MINIS

The Vintage Minis bring you the world's greatest writers on the experiences that make us human. These stylish, entertaining little books explore the whole spectrum of life – from birth to death, and everything in between. Which means there's something here for everyone, whatever your story.

vintageminis.co.uk